C000184100

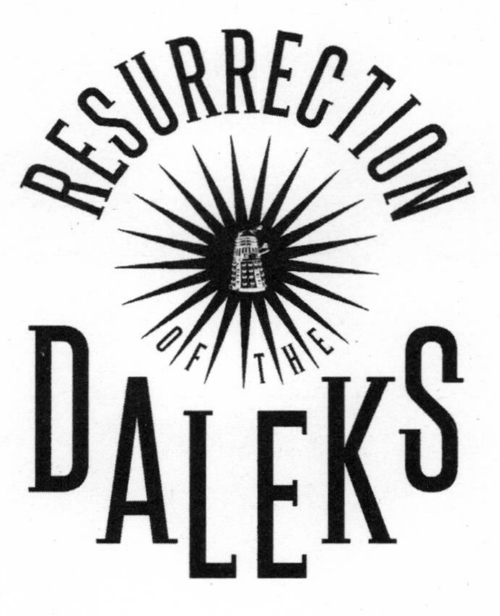
BBC
DOCTOR WHO
RESURRECTION
OF THE
DALEKS

BBC

DOCTOR WHO

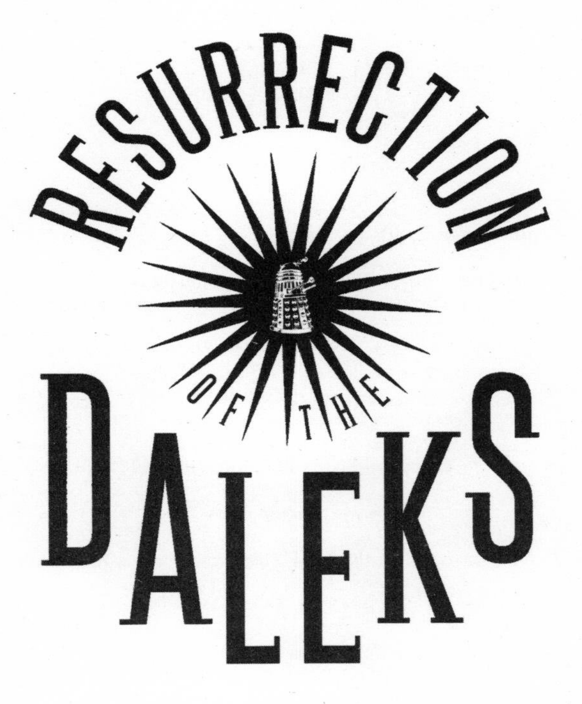

ERIC SAWARD

1 3 5 7 9 10 8 6 4 2

BBC Books, an imprint of Ebury Publishing
20 Vauxhall Bridge Road,
London SW1V 2SA

BBC Books is part of the Penguin Random House group of companies whose addresses can be found at global.penguinrandomhouse.com

Doctor Who is a BBC Wales production for BBC One.
Executive producers: Chris Chibnall and Matt Strevens

First published by BBC Books in 2019

www.penguin.co.uk

A CIP catalogue record for this book is available from the British Library

ISBN 9781785944338

Publishing Director: Albert DePetrillo
Project Editor: Steve Cole
Cover design: Two Associates
Production: Sian Pratley

Typeset in 10.5/13.13 pt Albertina MT Std
by Integra Software Services Pvt. Ltd, Pondicherry

Printed and bound in Great Britain by Clays Ltd, Elcograf S.p.A.

Penguin Random House is committed to a sustainable future for our business, our readers and our planet. This book is made from Forest Stewardship Council® certified paper.

Contents

For JJ, with all my love

Chapter One

The TARDIS rolled and tumbled helplessly in the bleakness of space. Barely conscious, the Doctor, his mind in a scramble, was laid out on the console room's floor trying to work out what to do next. Nearby, propped up against the wall, were his stunned companions, Tegan and Turlough.

Even in his current, shattered state, the Doctor could hear the near silent time bubbles popping in the stabilising dampers. If not corrected, the TARDIS risked being back-flipped in time and sent spiralling to the outer regions of oblivion.

If lucky, the time machine's engine would turn supernova resulting in the instant death of the Time Lord and his companions.

If unlucky, the TARDIS could become permanently trapped in a crack in time, causing the Doctor, and his two friends, to relive the same single moment over and over again. With the Doctor's regenerative powers still functioning, he would be condemned to a permanent state of living hell.

As the Doctor slipped into unconsciousness, it became apparent there was only one thing certain ...

The greatest Time Lord of them all was having a really bad day.

With walls like a smooth canyon, the Victorian group of buildings known as Butler's Wharf stretched almost languidly into the sky. Situated on the south bank of the River Thames, just east of Tower Bridge, the structure was completed in 1873. Reputedly the world's largest set of warehouses, the now deserted buildings had once stored much of the tea brought to Britain from around the world.

Behind Butler's Wharf was Shad Thames. By some, it is said to be a corruption of 'St John-at-Thames', a church which once stood nearby. Others say it was named after the shad, a fish, common to the area. Whatever, it was now a dingy service road that wove its way through the complex. High above the road, crisscrossing between the various structures, were several iron bridges once used for moving goods between buildings. Much damaged by neglect, these bridges now seemed to cling to the warehouse walls like frail fingers desperate to maintain a grip on some sort of reality. Once busy with the clatter of horses' hooves and the echo of many languages, the Shad Thames of 1984 was now devoid of all sound and activity ... except that of torrential rain.

Whipped up by a strong wind, the downpour lashed the road. Broken downpipes, precariously hanging from the warehouse walls, gurgled and spluttered, while drains backed up as they attempted to cope with the flood of water. As the deluge continued, Mr Jones, a forlorn-looking man in his late sixties, shuffled into Shad Thames. With his appearance as shabby and neglected as the surrounding edifices, he made his way uncertainly along the cracked pavement.

Having spent the night sleeping rough, Mr Jones had been caught by the inclement weather as he made his way to a local café. There, in exchange for a cooked breakfast, he would happily clean or do odd jobs. This was a routine he found more than equitable. But today, with an icy wind biting into him and a sodden overcoat that had started to leak, he decided it would be more expedient to postpone his journey until the storm ceased. Now in need of somewhere to shelter, he shuffled to the nearest warehouse and pressed his hand gingerly against the door. Finding it unlocked he pushed it open and surreptitiously slipped inside. A moment later he was safely ensconced in the entrance just behind the covered doorway.

With the noisome odour of a previous visitor still lingering, the area was at least dry and free from the wind. Feeling better, but still in need of restoring his shattered equilibrium, Mr Jones rummaged deep inside a pocket of his overcoat and withdrew an ancient tobacco tin. Carefully easing it open, he pulled out a cigarette paper and then unravelled enough tobacco to make the size of smoke he wanted. Once the cigarette had been fully assembled, he nonchalantly popped it into his mouth, took out an ancient lighter and, with its distinctive *clink*, flipped open the lid.

Momentarily mindful that cigarette smoking was considered an unpleasant and dangerous habit, he nevertheless gave the lighter's thumbwheel a sharp flick and sent it spinning against its flint. Even though producing a worthy pyrotechnic display of sparks, the wick's ignition remained elusive.

Undeterred he tried again, but instead of the desired flame there was a sudden and almighty crash from somewhere outside the warehouse.

Startled, Mr Jones pushed the door ajar and peered out. Twenty yards away, through oblique shafts of heavy rain, he could see a massive warehouse door had been thrown open. Two men had stepped cautiously into the road, dressed in shabby, powder-blue jumpsuits, with insignia on their shoulders and the names 'Stien' and 'Galloway' respectively stitched above their left breast pockets. Mr Jones rightly assumed they were soldiers. Although he didn't know from where they had come, he couldn't but help notice how tired and exhausted they looked. Even slamming the warehouse door seemed to take an enormous effort, but not as much as when they started to lollop along Shad Thames in the direction of Mr Jones.

Fearing an assault, he pressed himself deeper into the sepulchral gloom of his doorway. With the soldiers almost parallel with his hiding place, Mr Jones raised his untrained fists in a gesture of self-defence. But instead of attacking him the soldiers jogged by at the precise moment the warehouse door, this time accompanied by a chorus of human shouts and screams, was again kicked open …

The Battle of Shad Thames was far from over.

As the two soldiers ducked into a doorway further up the road, Mr Jones looked in the direction of the turmoil and saw, pouring out of the warehouse, a group of terrified men and women. Discombobulated, they desperately milled around until three uniformed policemen, two of whom were armed with machine pistols, also pushed their way from the warehouse and into the road. On seeing the guns, and fearing the inevitable, the group, now screaming even louder, began to run for their lives.

Without hesitation, the armed constables levelled their weapons and, in short controlled bursts, started to fire. As the muted sound of discharging weapons reverberated around the tall buildings, bullets ripped into bodies. First one, then another hit the rain-drenched road with a sickening thud. This was followed by more gunfire and yet further people dying. Even Mr Jones, standing in his doorway, traumatised by events, had been shot. Caught by a stray bullet, and with the same unlit cigarette still between his lips, a man who had never harmed anyone slid down the warehouse wall and died.

With twenty bodies strewn along the road, the police constables moved quickly among their victims, attaching a transporter module to each corpse.

The third policeman, who was dressed as a 1980s police inspector and unarmed, watched as the constables diligently worked without a flicker of concern or emotion. When they had finished, the police inspector slipped a small, silver box from his pocket and pressed the slide control on its side. With a high-pitched whine, and a slight incandescent glow of the box, everyone, except the two constables, slowly dissolved from sight.

With the street empty, the policemen brushed down their coats and checked their helmets were on straight. Then, as though the slaughter of so many people was of little significance, they casually strolled off along the road, under the iron bridges, past the Old Custom House and on towards the Victorian marvel that was Tower Bridge.

Even with the policemen gone and the rain starting to ease, Shad Thames continued to maintain a grim countenance. As though infected by the mood of the road, Sergeant Stien attempted to relieve the throbbing pain in his back by wedging himself up against the doorway wall. 'W-w-where do you think the policemen have gone?' he stammered.

'Patrolling …' muttered Galloway. 'Making sure no one discovers what's in the warehouse.'

Cautiously, Stien peered along the road. 'You're saying they'll b-b-be back?'

Galloway nodded. 'Which means, if we're to stay alive, we will have to kill them.'

Stien didn't like the sound of that, but then he never liked anything to do with violence, especially when it affected him. Short and squat, he was a nervous man who often stuttered in moments of fear or tension. Far from being a naturally talented soldier, he displayed, when it came to logistics, a decided perspicacity which had led to the army making him a quartermaster sergeant. Although in charge of distributing the apparatus of war, he himself had always managed to avoid armed confrontation. This, as he now realised, might have been a mistake, especially as he was now being asked to fight two highly egregious policemen.

'We need to get away from here,' said Stien, as he pulled himself upright. 'I'm not up for a fight, not with the state of m-m-my back.'

Galloway was tired of hearing Stien play the coward. 'We need to get back to the others, let them know what happened here.'

'We can't f-f-fight those p-p-policemen!' said Stien, his stammer noticeably worse. 'We're *unarmed*!'

But Galloway was no longer listening. 'We must do our duty,' he said firmly. 'You're a soldier. Prove your loyalty to those with whom we serve.' Not waiting for a response, he strode off along Shad Thames.

'It's all right for you,' Stien shouted after him, 'but I'm not combat trained. I can't afford your s-s-sort of principles!'

Instead of replying, Galloway, with sudden renewed energy, broke into a jog. On seeing how quickly he was moving, and concerned he might be left behind, Stien scampered after him. 'Even if we avoid our two policemen,' he panted, 'there could be others, in the warehouse … *w-w-waiting*!'

But Galloway wasn't in the mood for defeatist talk. As he continued to pound the pavement, the need to win already filling his mind, all Stien could do was puff along behind. He too would have loved to share Galloway's fantasy of a gallant victory, but all that crackled across his synapses was a sense of instant doom where both men were murdered in a grotesquely, undignified manner.

For Sergeant Stien, the Battle for Shad Thames wasn't going at all well.

Somewhere, in the sector known as the Hyperion Delta, Zone Four, an enormous battlecruiser hung motionless in space. Except for a shaft of white light, emanating from a high point on the ship's superstructure, the cruiser was in darkness. Although the beam appeared to be little more than an over-bright navigation lamp, its real purpose was far more dangerous. Much like a laser beam, the finger of light was designed to cut through the enormity of space until, at a prearranged point, gravity would take over and force the light to spiral and twist its way through the cracks and fissures in the time-space continuum. As pressure built, and the light became more compressed, the contracting beam was transmogrified into the swirling mass of a time corridor. With one end connected to the cruiser docked in Earth calendar year 4590, and the other to the warehouse at Shad Thames in 1984, travel between the two points in time was possible.

In spite of the battlecruiser's mighty presence, aboard ship was very different. Small and compact, the interior had been divided into surprisingly tight, uncluttered work areas. Corridors, with their low, curved ceilings were difficult for a fully grown humanoid male to stand upright. The same compactness even applied to the ship's bridge. With its massive warp engine controls and advanced navigation system, there seemed hardly enough space for the ship's company to perform their duties. Not until the cruiser's controls were examined did it become apparent they weren't designed for use by a crew with prehensile hands. That was because it was a Dalek ship and Daleks do not have hands – prehensile or otherwise.

On a floor above the bridge, where the time corridor connected to the cruiser, was a receiving chamber where items transported through the corridor would emerge. Juxtaposed to the chamber was a docking area where goods were held until allocated their place on board. Separating the two units was an enormous airlock designed to prevent undesirable objects entering the main body of the ship. For added security, two Troopers were also stationed there.

Scratching behind his ear, the senior Trooper examined the small screen on the control panel at the side of the airlock. 'There's activity,' he muttered to the second Trooper. 'The time corridor is operational.'

Quickly he inserted the inbound clearance code. 'Incoming goods.' He operated a switch on the control panel and the low sibilant noise of the time suppressors kicked in. That was followed by the whine of gravity giros revving up to full speed. 'It's arrived,' said the senior Trooper softly. 'The package has arrived.'

As the airlock door slowly slid open, the two Troopers snapped to attention. Standing in the time chamber, surrounded by the bodies of those killed in Shad Thames, was the police inspector. In reality, the inspector was a military commander called Gustav Lytton.

'That was a shambles,' Lytton snarled. 'What went wrong?'

'Sir, the escape was prevented, *sir!*' The senior Trooper shouted the word '*sir!*' in the stylised, staccato fashion used when addressing officers. 'All prisoners are accounted for, *sir!*'

'They got out of the warehouse,' Lytton snarled. 'It should never have happened!'

'Sir, no, *sir!*'

'And who ordered the use of machine pistols?'

'Standing orders, *sir!* Nothing anachronistic is to be taken to Earth, *sir!*'

Snatching the police inspector's hat from his head, Lytton hurled it across the room. 'So instead we slaughter valuable specimens!'

'An unfortunate error, *sir!* Although two escapees are still free and unharmed, *sir!*'

Lytton nodded, as he removed his police inspector's jacket, 'My men will deal with those.'

'Sir, yes, *sir!*'

'Just remember,' added Lytton, 'next time stun lasers are to be used. If not, the next execution squad will be coming for you.'

'Sir, yes, *sir!*'

Lytton pointed at the hat and jacket. 'Now pick them up and get out of my sight.'

'Sir, yes, *sir!*'

With the Troopers gone, Lytton ducked beneath the low lintel of the time chamber and entered the docking area. He was far from happy. A serious mistake had been made in a situation where none could be afforded. Lytton had not just a difficult adversary, but also a ferocious employer: Daleks didn't like blunders but, unlike Lytton, they had the habit of slaughtering those responsible without justice, interrogation or remorse. Lytton knew that he could easily meet a similar fate.

Back in Shad Thames, Galloway and Stien had cautiously re-entered the warehouse from where they had earlier escaped. Silently they made their way up the dark, wooden stairs and into an empty storage area. After allowing their eyes to adjust to the low level of light, they started to look around. Even with its enormous floor space, the low ceilings and cast-iron pillars made the area feel cramped and claustrophobic. Neither was their search helped by the amount of debris scattered over the floor. Largely made up of broken tea chests, in various states of decay, the detritus gave off an unpleasant dust as the two soldiers shuffled around. Elsewhere, piles of empty sacks were strewn around as though having been used by people sleeping rough. Somewhere else was a pile of old newspapers and lengths of timber.

Along the outside wall of the warehouse was a large service door. This led to a wall-mounted crane once used to lift chests of tea into the warehouse. Next to the door was a massive window – more suited to a church. Coated in so much grime, little light could enter through it.

With their search having taken them to the middle of the floor, Galloway bent to examine two larger pieces of tea chest positioned adjacent to each other. Poking around in the debris, he selected a large piece.

Stien was confused. 'I thought we were s-searching for the time corridor?'

Galloway nodded. 'And I think we've found it.' Turning over one of the chests, he pointed at a line of teeny numbers running along one of its metal-reinforced corner seams. 'That may look like a pencil-written warehouse code, but I'd say it was a computer readout.'

Tentatively, Stien rubbed a finger over the smooth numbers and then felt even more confused. 'Why a c-c-computer in a tea chest?'

'They're markers to indicate where the time corridor joins the warehouse. They also stabilise the corridor's entrance by locking it onto the time-space continuum.'

Stien guffawed. 'A time corridor is state-of-the-art science. They don't have t-t-tat like this as entry markers.'

Climbing to his feet, Galloway indicated the remnants of the broken chests around them. 'Look at this place,' he said prodding at the debris with the toe of his boot. 'An empty tea chest couldn't be less incongruous.'

Still uncertain it was a live display panel, Stien stared at the readout. Then, in search of the computer, he closely examined the interior of the chest, but found nothing. It wasn't until his eye once again caught sight of the readout that he noticed some of the numbers had changed. As he continued to look, two more of the digits suddenly blinked and altered. 'You're right,' he muttered. '*This thing is live.*'

Galloway looked at the readout – suddenly the numbers changed. 'That's bad news,' he said. 'Someone's using the corridor.' From the floor he quickly snatched up a length of timber and held it up in front of him like a quarterstaff. 'We need to get out of here!'

With Galloway acting as a rearguard, a terrified Stien crashed through the landing door, leapt down too many steps at once and only came to a halt when reaching the heavy-duty door of the warehouse. Expecting Galloway to be close behind, Stien was surprised to find himself alone. Realising something was wrong, he glanced up the stairs and quietly called Galloway's name, but instead of a reply there was a distant, short burst of a machine pistol . . .

Up on the first floor of the warehouse, one of Lytton's black-clad Troopers stood over the dead body of Galloway. Bending down, she clipped a transporter module onto the deceased man's tunic, took out a silver box and pressed the slide control. With a high-pitched whine, and a slight incandescent glow of the box, both Galloway and the Trooper dissolved into the swirling mists of the time corridor.

CHAPTER TWO

Somewhere, far, far away, a time machine continued to have problems. As a consequence, the Time Lord and his companions had fortunately been jerked out of their unconsciousness much as the TARDIS had fallen out of time. One moment it had been slipping and sliding through the cracks in time, the next it had hurtled into a colossal hole in the space-time continuum. Now being pushed to its limits, the TARDIS engines had started to roar like some giant, prehistoric creature. As the G-force in the console room had continued to rise, Tegan and Turlough had been helplessly flattened against the floor, while the Doctor, now clinging to the console's pedestal, desperately struggled to regain control of the time machine.

'Time spillage,' the Doctor grunted. 'And it's getting worse.'

As the Time Lord eased his way down the console's pedestal, he knew he had to do something positive before he passed out again. With enormous effort, the Doctor managed to kick open a hatch at the base of the pedestal that covered the manual override for the time stabilisers. As Tegan and Turlough once more verged on unconsciousness, the Doctor painfully made his way down to the opening. With leaden fingers, he pulled at the controls, but nothing happened. Summoning all his strength, he tugged again but it still refused to budge. Realising he must generate more leverage, the Doctor knew he would have to exploit the additional force generated by the spinning room. This meant releasing the hold his entwined legs had around the pedestal and allowing his body to swing out like a gondola on an out-of-control merry-go-round. The reality was that if his grip failed it would mean the immediate death of all on board and the inevitable destruction of the TARDIS. Aware there was no other choice, the Doctor carefully locked his fingers around the controls and, satisfied his grip was the strongest possible, slowly released his legs. Pain tore through his arms and shoulders as his body snapped rigid under the strain, but his grip held, and – slowly, very slowly – the controls began to move and the time stabilisers took effect . . .

It was almost an hour after the room had ceased spinning that the Doctor and his companions summoned up the strength to move.

'So *that's* time spillage,' said Turlough, attempting to sound ultra-cool.

The Doctor slipped on his half-framed spectacles and examined one of the small computer screens. 'Unfortunately, the spillage is a large one, hence we're still trapped in the gravitational drag.'

Tegan wasn't happy. 'There's always some excuse. Can't we just materialise and escape from it that way?'

The Time Lord shook his head and crawled over to join her. 'At our current speed, we'd risk breaking up.'

As Tegan's face crumpled into a look of anguish, the Doctor placed a reassuring arm around her shoulder. 'Don't worry,' he said. 'We'll soon be free of the corridor. We just have to wait for the right moment.' He smiled like a benevolent uncle. 'Trust me, it will all come out right very soon.'

But on this occasion, the Doctor was mistaken.

With a sudden, spine-cracking lurch, Tegan and Turlough were once again hurled across the console room. To make things worse, the Cloister Bell, the TARDIS's ominous herald of doom, started to sound. Although Tegan knew little about how the time machine worked, she did know the importance of the Campana Magna, and that its toll indicated the imminent destruction of the TARDIS.

Welcome Aboard the Vipod More
The Most Hated Facility in the Solar System.

This had been scratched above Airlock Three of the *Vipod Mor*. Who had written it was unknown. The author of the message had also deliberately misspelt the word '*Mor*'. Why they had done this was another mystery. The only certain thing was that the entire crew of eighty-three were unhappy and didn't want to be where they were.

Things hadn't always been like this.

In the old days, things had been calmer.

In the old days, the *Vipod Mor* had been a battlecruiser that had fought bravely and with honour in the Hexicon Delta Zone Wars. In those days, the ship was known as the *Fighting Brigand* and was captained by Anthony Smyth, a tough, rumbustious space captain known for his ability to quaff vast amounts of Voxnic, the brew, not unlike absinthe, known to have undone many a loyal and gallant man.

After Smyth's retirement, the ship was given to Fellion Vipod Mor, poet, explorer, scientist and lover. It was a relationship with the Admiral's domestic droid – a creature of stunning beauty and utterly deep understanding – that lost him everything. Found in the wrong time and a very wrong place, his punishment was to be sealed in his own vessel and left to drift in space. This he did for ninety-seven years.

After Fellion's demise, the cruiser was recommissioned, this time as a proper prison ship and, with an amazing lack of imagination, named the *Vipod Mor*. Aboard this ship was placed a very special prisoner, a creature so dangerous it could never be released.

Although the exterior of the *Vipod Mor* looked bleak, the interior was even worse. The crew had almost entirely given up on any form of procedure, maintenance or discipline ...

That was except for a new recruit to the *Vipod Mor* – Lieutenant Tyler Mercer. Bright but unintentionally arrogant, Mercer, the new Head of Security, strutted along the ill-lit central corridor. Since the age of twenty, Mercer had been in Space Intelligence. Although now twenty-eight, and too old for combat duty, his new appointment made him the youngest Head of Security in the Intergalactic Penitentiary Service. Yet in spite of his success in Intelligence, and his advanced training in deep-space hyper-navigation, Tyler Mercer was lost in the Facility he was currently employed to keep secure.

Angry with himself for having made such a foolish mistake, Mercer turned abruptly into a side corridor and almost collided with Dr Elizabeth Styles, the Facility's Medical Officer.

'Look where you're going,' she snapped.

While he couldn't fully disregard her unfriendly tone, neither could Mercer ignore her innate attractiveness and the pure serendipity of their meeting. Dressed in a spotless, white uniform, she was tall and athletic with a strong, symmetrical face topped by a beautifully cut head of fiery red hair. Even without Mercer's rapidly growing sense of lasciviousness, he was convinced she was the most attractive woman he had seen since leaving Star Base Control. Yet, in spite of his efforts to convey the sensuality of his feeling, Styles wasn't interested. Instead she turned her scowl up to maximum and said: 'And you are?'

'Tyler Mercer,' he replied, executing what he considered was his sexiest *cute-as-a-button* salute. 'And for the last two days I've been the Facility's new Head of Security.'

Styles's face crumpled even more. 'I'd heard there was a new one,' she said, 'although I never expected to find him lurking around here.'

Mercer decided to risk a small smile. '*Howie Kellim,*' he said, using the formal Star Fleet greeting.

'*Howie Kellim Bi,*' Styles replied with utter indifference.

'Actually, I was looking for you,' said Mercer, pointing at her name badge. 'I'm spending the next day or two getting to know senior members of the team.'

Styles still wasn't impressed. 'There's nothing of interest about me,' she said. 'My duty is simply to look after the physical and psychological wellbeing of the Prisoner, the crew and the ship's cat.'

Mercer allowed her sentence to hang in the air for a moment. 'Actually, apart from meeting people, I've also been observing the general chaos of the Facility.' He indicated a mass of cables hanging from an inspection panel. 'This sort of neglect is everywhere.'

Styles shrugged, turned and strolled back along the corridor. 'If you want spick 'n' span,' she said over her shoulder, 'never get transferred to a prison ship located on the edge of oblivion.'

'That's hardly the point,' said Mercer, catching up with her. 'Standards should be higher than this.' He pointed at the corridor's overhead lamps. 'Look at it. There's hardly enough light to see where we're going.'

Styles snorted as she came to a sudden stop. 'Maybe the Facility is better viewed in the dark.'

Having reached her laboratory, Styles stood in front of the door and placed a hand over a wall-mounted pressure plate. 'ID confirmed,' a highly camp computer-generated voice purred. 'Welcome, Dr Elizabeth Styles. As always, a pleasure to serve you.'

With a gentle whirring noise, the door slid open and Mercer followed Styles into the pristine lab.

'Very cosy,' he said looking around. 'And so beautifully clean.'

'That's down to my nurse. Say, hello to the new Head of Security, Monda.'

'*Guten Tag, mein Herr.*'

'She's speaking German.'

'Well observed. If you come back next month it will be Terileptil. I'm keen to improve my languages.'

Mercer looked at Monda and realised how amazingly beautiful she was. '*Howie Kellim,*' he said in an excessively unctuous tone. Mercer couldn't believe there were two beautiful women in the same room on board the same Facility!

'I wouldn't get too excited,' said Styles. 'Monda is an android.'

Mercer couldn't do anything but stare. Monda was stunning. How did they manufacture such amazingly lifelike creatures?

'Neither do you greet droids with the "*Howie Kellim*".'

'Yes, I know,' said Mercer. 'It just seemed the right thing to do.' Suddenly remembering the problems that Fellion Vipod Mor had experienced with the Admiral's domestic droid, Mercer switched his full attention back to Styles. 'With such an immaculate laboratory,' he said trying to sound as though he still really cared, 'it must be hard coping with the mess elsewhere.'

'That's easy,' she said. 'I simply ignore everything that doesn't affect me.'

Even though Mercer was trying hard to adjust to Styles' casual style of communication, her reply irritated him more than he expected. 'The morale on this Facility is appalling,' he said. 'Surely, as Medical Officer, it's your duty to see something is done?'

Styles was getting tired of Mercer's criticism. 'Look,' she said, 'the crew and the Prisoner are healthy. The ship's cat, who is called Sir Runcible, is also well fed. What else do you expect?'

Slipping on a sterilised gown, Styles crossed to her workstation, sat down in front of a video microscope and fiddled with the controls. 'My tour of duty ends in a few weeks. Unfortunately, for a promotion, I'm dependent on a good report from the Captain.' She suddenly bit her bottom lip as though reminding herself not to say too much. 'If I publicly criticise the state of the Facility, I would also be broadcasting my disapproval of the officer in charge. That means I would be unlikely to get a transfer and could be stuck here for another five mind-numbing years!'

At the thought of her near-imprisonment, Styles's face tightened with anger and a single tear silently ran down her cheek. Although Mercer felt sorry for Styles, and would like to have offered some sort of emotional support, all he could manage were a few muttered clichés. His lack of insensitivity annoyed him. It also made him wonder, with so much emotional tension present, how long he would be able to cope with life on board the *Vipod Mor*.

*

On 1984 Earth, Sergeant Stien was also feeling confused. Perched on an iron bridge connecting two of the warehouses, he stared at the wet road nearly four metres below. With Galloway dead, Stien was now trapped on an alien planet with little chance of escape. Even if it were safe to use the time corridor, the technical aspects were way beyond his skills. What with armed policemen patrolling the local streets and Troopers lurking in the night-black shadows of the warehouse, his life seemed near to its end.

With the rain still falling, Stien crouched behind a sheet of corrugated iron that had been fitted to the bridge's handrail as a homemade windbreak. Completely drenched, and now ravenously hungry, he wondered where he could obtain food. Without money he would be unable to buy any. Neither could he steal it as his powder-blue uniform, emblazoned with name and rank, would hardly maintain his anonymity.

As Stien continued to review his situation, a plain white, fifteen-hundredweight van sped into Shad Thames and screeched to a halt. Colonel Archer, Sergeant Calder and Professor Laird quickly scrambled from the cab of the van while two soldiers jumped out of the open double doors at the back. All, except Professor Laird, were dressed in British military combat uniforms and carried automatic weapons.

While Laird and the others ran into the warehouse, Sergeant Calder retrieved a small holdall from inside the cab. He then slammed the door and banged on the van's side indicating it was safe to pull away. Obeying, and with yet more screeching of tyres, the vehicle rapidly accelerated along Shad Thames, rounded a surprisingly sharp corner and was gone. Having watched it depart, Calder then silently followed in his colleagues' footsteps, into the warehouse.

Still observing from his hiding place, a puzzled Stien wondered whether the recently arrived group had anything to do with the time corridor or the black-suited Troopers who supervised it. More to the point he wanted to know, given the growing tension, how long it would be before the two groups met and yet more people died.

Suddenly a large globule of water separated from a gutter high up on the building, rolled and tumbled through the air before smacking into the back of the Stien's neck. Although he was already completely drenched, the impact was surprisingly vindictive, as though someone, somewhere, was trying to make him feel that little bit more uncomfortable.

It had worked. Stien was now truly unhappy.

On the ground floor of the warehouse, one of the soldiers unlocked a door mounted beneath the main staircase and pushed it open. Taking a torch from his holdall, Calder switched it on and shone the beam into the cupboard's darkness. Finding the light switches, he turned them on and, a moment later, several portable floodlights crackled into action in the cellar.

Avoiding the use of the rickety banister, the group carefully descended the twelve steps to the basement and, on arrival, lodged their weapons in a security rack.

Although the cellar had been furnished in a makeshift manner, judicious scrounging from local builders' skips had provided a surprisingly attractive hoard of furniture. In the middle of the room stood a slightly scratched G-plan dining table and six chairs. On the other side of the room there was a low-level cupboard from Henrik's. Perched on its top was a combination microwave cooker, an electric kettle and everything necessary for making tea, including – amazingly – half a dozen unchipped, matching mugs. Scattered around the room were several easy chairs, a camp bed and an assortment of surprisingly sophisticated reading material borrowed from the local library. In many respects, the area looked like a well-to-do student's bedroom except for one thing: in a corner, there was a low-level blast wall surrounding a shallow trench. At the bottom of the excavation were six ribbed, matt-black cylinders approximately seventy centimetres long. Whether they were bombs, dropped in the Second World War, or oxyacetylene bottles buried by an irresponsible builder, bomb disposal experts Major Archer and Sergeant Calder, with the aid of metallurgist Professor Laird, would find out.

But, before that activity could continue, a ritual had first to be observed. Crossing to the low-level cupboard, Sergeant Calder opened his holdall and removed several packets of sandwiches, an assortment of biscuits and a carton of fresh milk.

'I think we need a brew, Lance Corporal Miller,' he said to one of the soldiers. 'You can't defuse bombs when you're parched.' Sergeant Calder always said the same thing when he asked for tea to be made. Although the team no longer found his remark funny, they still smiled out of a sense of camaraderie.

Little did they know it would be the last time they would hear him speak those words.

In the console room, with the time rotor barely oscillating, the Doctor was still hunting for an effective way to break free from the corridor. During his search, and quite by accident, he had found an almost subliminal line of computer code on one of the console's smaller screens. Even though its appearance was brief, the Doctor realised there was something familiar about it, something from the past …

But why didn't he recognise it now?

As he set the computer to search for the code's source, the Time Lord also noticed that some of the pressure readings, unaltered for decades, had changed on the TARDIS controls.

Quickly, the Doctor crossed to one of the many roundels that covered the wall of the console room and levered open its translucent cover. Inside was a mass of densely packed electronics. The Doctor once again took out his half-framed glasses, popped them onto his nose and closely examined the contents of the roundel. Nodding sagely, as though familiar with every piece of equipment, he thrust his hand into a spaghetti ball-like profusion of electronics. Instead of finding the component for which he was searching, his hand was suddenly bombarded by a peripatetic bolt of high-voltage electricity. Grimacing, he quickly extracted his hand from the roundel. Even though there wasn't anyone in the room, he continued to pretend nothing had happened and that he was fully in control.

'Everything OK?' said Tegan, entering the console room.

'Couldn't be better,' he lied. 'In fact, everything is spiffing, top hole. Once I've stabilised the pulse coils, reset the vacuum ratios and rebooted the semi-conductors, everything should be, well, like me ... much calmer.'

'Does that mean we can get away from here? Maybe go somewhere *safe*?'

'Not quite,' said the Doctor. 'Apart from the sudden and unexpected changes in the controls, I also need to know why the corridor is following a timeline to 1984 Earth.'

Tegan scowled. 'After what we've been through we need to get away, not get further involved.'

But the Doctor had other things on his mind. Smiling to himself, he removed a wooden HP pencil from an inside pocket. 'Trapping the TARDIS in the corridor,' he said, 'was not only deliberate, but required enormous skill in time manipulation.' Casually, the Doctor rammed the pencil into a small hole in a circuit board and started to wiggle it about. 'I now need to know who is capable of such time manipulation, why they are building time corridors for me to fall into and what else they are intending to do.' He continued to work the pencil even harder until, without warning, the circuit board separated from its connections to reveal the time compressor lodged beneath.

'Ah, there we are,' the Time Lord muttered, as though addressing a pet cat. 'Daddy's got you, little one.' The Doctor plunged the pencil back into his pocket. 'Once I've rebooted the compressor, things should ... well, quieten down.'

As Tegan waited for the Doctor to carry out what she thought would be some highly adroit manipulation, he instead drew back his arm and punched the compressor as hard as he could. 'That should stabilise things nicely,' he muttered as he slotted the circuit board back in place, closed the roundel's cover and returned to the console.

Tegan was stunned by the Time Lord's crudeness. 'Are you sure you know what you're doing? Beating up electronics may be fashionable on Gallifrey but how will it explain why the time corridor is going to 1984 Earth?'

The Doctor jabbed a finger at a small screen mounted on the console. 'At this very moment the TARDIS is hacking data from the extremities of the corridor's computer. That's how I can tell you our destination is 1984 London. Meanwhile the suppressors are stabilising the time turbulence created by the drag of the corridor. Hence why we are no longer crashing into power dives every few minutes.'

'Sure,' said Tegan, 'but what if the corridor's computer knows you've tapped into it?'

A smile wound its way across the Doctor's face. 'I don't think so,' he said, a little too knowingly. 'It's too busy supervising its own activities to notice my peripheral tinkering ...'

But, once again, the Doctor was mistaken. Deep inside the corridor, its principal computer was, as Tegan had predicted, more than aware something had penetrated its system. Poised, ready to counter-attack, it waited for the right moment. Like most machines built for war it had, as the Doctor was about to find out, a very aggressive way of dealing with intruders.

CHAPTER THREE

Aboard the *Vipod Mor*, Tyler Mercer, Head of Security, entered the main control room. In one corner, her feet resting on the fascia of an enormous radio transceiver, was Ensign Fabian Osborn. In touch with the whole Facility, including the patrolling starfighters, Osborn was the 'ears' of the unit. Sharp and intelligent, she spent much of her time translating Terileptil poetry into Northern Hemisphere Earth English, the preferred language of all true poets.

In another part of the room, lounging in front of the deep-space scanner, was Senior Ensign 'Baz' Seaton. Seeming to spend endless hours staring blankly at the machine before him, it was difficult to appreciate precisely what he was registering. To some of the crew he was considered one of the dimmest people aboard. That was until a recent computer glitch had mistakenly caused the crew's personnel files to be published. This revealed, much to some people's irritation, that Seaton not only had the highest IQ of the crew, but also had a PhD in astrophysics and another entitled 'Dark Matter contra the Time-Space Continuum'. To make things even worse, Seaton was also an inspired cook and his pop-up dinner parties were now famous. In spite of all this, the reasons for him being in such a lowly position aboard the prison ship remained a secret.

As Mercer crossed the control deck, he had foolishly hoped the Ensigns might salute the *Howie Kellim*. But all that happened was Osborn gave him a friendly wave and indicated he should come and sit with her.

'I saw your look of disappointment,' she said, as Mercer lowered himself into an adjacent chair, 'but we no longer salute in this section of the Facility.' And, as though offering a tiny modicum of consolation, she smiled broadly revealing a perfect set of beautiful teeth. 'The no-saluting stuff usually upsets most of the newly promoted officers, but they soon get over it, especially when they realise that so much of what they learned at the Academy just doesn't apply here.'

Mercer almost sighed. Still wishing to make the rank of Captain by the age of thirty, he knew that meant a lot of hard work. He also knew, because of the negativity that dominated the *Vipod Mor*, he would find progress very difficult indeed.

Tegan brought a stool from her room and placed it in front of the console. While Turlough had gone off to check for damage in other parts of the TARDIS – he liked nothing better than a good skulk about – she wanted to learn more about the ship's controls and why the Doctor found them so difficult to operate. As she studied a scanner screen, a fine line of computer code flickered across a monitor. 'Look,' she called. 'There's more of this hieroglyph stuff.'

Irritated by the interruption, the Doctor crossed to where Tegan was seated. 'You see this,' she said pointing at the screen. 'What does that mean?'

As the Doctor considered the situation, he noticed his fingers had not only started to sting but he was also unable to focus on the jumble of images before they suddenly vanished. Although he had recognised the code as the one glimpsed earlier, he still couldn't remember what it was called. This annoyed him, as a strong sense of intuition was now hinting he had seen the code in another time, place and under very unpleasant circumstances.

Now seated on Tegan's stool, and with his mind focused on what he had to do, the Doctor started to search his own memories. With the Time Lord's unique ability for psychological self-examination, he metaphorically waded into his own mind. Arriving at his own hippocampus, the Doctor saw the memory of an old, wooden school box. With a hue as clear and pure as spring sunlight, it also possessed, like a lover's kiss, a tactile quality that comforted and reassured. Although glad to be reminded of the box's natural beauty, the Doctor was nevertheless surprised that of all the things that could have appeared it was a box he hadn't thought about for centuries. As the Doctor considered the situation, he noticed that not only had his fingers started to sting, but also that several of them had turned blue. With the box being the last thing touched, the Time Lord examined it more closely and noticed the dust on its lid had also changed. Without hesitation, the Doctor began to tear at the lid. Gone was the sensual, tactile quality of the wood, replaced now with a dry, crumbling substance. Although the Doctor had seen objects made from image transference before, he had never seen one of such fine quality.

With the lid destroyed, the Doctor looked inside. Twisting and writhing, like some demonic snake, was a much-enlarged section of the computer code. To make things even more unpleasant, a sudden, gratingly painful noise started to emanate from the box. Struggling to get away from the all-pervasive sound, the Doctor pushed himself back towards the way he had entered his mind. 'I've found it,' shouted the Doctor as he wrenched himself back into reality. However, the noise persisted.

Tegan and the Doctor clamped their hands protectively over their ears. As the noise grew louder, the Time Lord remembered he still had a few jelly babies left over from a previous regeneration. Rapidly, the Doctor inserted a hand into a pocket, produced two fluff-covered specimens and dropped them in Tegan's hand. He then found two more and rammed one into each ear. With their hearing protected, they quickly moved to the computer controls.

'I'm a fool!' the Doctor shouted, starting to snap off every switch on the console. 'I should never have set the TARDIS computer in search for the coding – it now thinks I'm attacking it.'

He knew they had to prevent the code from infecting the engines, causing negative phasing and turning the time machine into a floating morgue. 'Tegan, help me!'

Following the point of his finger, she scrambled beneath the console and switched off all the recently fitted JJ, Mk Two, circuit breakers.

In a last desperate attempt, the Doctor pulled a panel from the top of the console and rummaged frantically among the wiring and circuit boards inside. Having only the vaguest idea of what he was doing and little concept of the long-term effect his activities would have, the Doctor found himself hacking out a huge number of printed circuits, mounted Pearldek crystals and tinclavic-augmented fusion rods. At first nothing happened, but then ... slowly, very slowly, the Ciskinady code was locked out of the ship's computer and the ear-splitting noise started to fade. The Doctor had won. He was regaining control of his ship. With the noise gone, and the computer screens clear, the Doctor collected the jelly babies and returned them to his pocket.

Waste not, want not.

'What an utter mess,' said a familiar voice. Turning the Doctor saw Turlough, standing in the doorway and bringing his hands together in a slow, mocking handclap. 'Ciskinady coding,' Turlough sneered. 'That's really playing with the big boys, Doctor.'

'What's he talking about?' asked Tegan. 'What is with this Ciskinady code thing?'

'Tell her what's happening,' Turlough suggested. 'More to the point, tell her who's involved.'

The Time Lord closed his eyes as though trying to shut out a dreadful memory …

'Daleks,' he said at last.

Tegan looked puzzled. 'And what are Daleks?'

The Doctor shrugged and then explained how the Daleks were a race of ruthless mutants from the planet Skaro. How they were created by a crazed Kaled scientist named Davros, during a thousand-year war, and how he had genetically engineered living subjects and integrated them within a tank-like mechanical shell with a front-mounted, all-powerful gun. The resulting creatures were bent on universal conquest and were utterly without pity, compassion or remorse. Having had every emotion removed, except that of hate, it left them with an overwhelming desire to purge the universe of all non-Dalek life forms.

'How do you know they're involved?' Tegan demanded.

'It's the presence of the Ciskinady code,' the Doctor said. 'It's too complex for most beings. The Daleks are the only group who can use it.

Tegan scowled. 'Why didn't you tell me about these Daleks before?'

The Doctor thought for a moment. 'I didn't mean to keep it secret,' he said. 'Maybe it was because I thought the Daleks had been destroyed.' There was now a tone of desperation in his voice. 'If they are back, as the Ciskinady code suggests, we can expect nothing but slaughter and destruction. In which case, it's my duty to hunt them down and, this time, eradicate them forever.'

His voice trailed away and the room was silent other than for the time rotor gently oscillating…

Tegan and Turlough exchanged furtive glances. Turlough's earlier smugness was gone. They had never before heard the Doctor talk in such a vehement manner, especially about killing. For once the companions chose not to argue as, this time, they sensed the Time Lord meant precisely what he had said.

At the Earth year 4590 end of the time corridor, the Dalek battlecruiser started to move. The shaft of white light, emanating from high up on the ship's superstructure, still shone. Although the cruiser was mainly in darkness, fizzles of blue light skittered across the ship's hull. This was caused by the already active force field present to protect the cruiser when travelling at warp speed or under attack.

Up on the ship's bridge there was a mass of activity. Although there were two Daleks in attendance, the pre-flight procedures were mainly undertaken by a Tellurian crew. Dressed in cream uniforms, they worked carefully and precisely, checking the status of every function aboard the vessel.

On the far side of the bridge, standing in front of a large scanner-screen, was Commander Lytton. Supervising his own pre-flight routine, he watched as ribbons of information flashed across his screen.

With the sound of the engines building and the speed of the cruiser rapidly increasing, Lytton watched as the vital functions of the vessel came together like a living organism. Lytton was not a very emotional man and rarely displayed signs of excitement. Even when he shouted at a crewmember, it was usually for effect rather than a heightened state of emotion. In fact, the nearest Lytton ever came to displaying any sense of feeling was when, as commander of a battlecruiser, he was able to give what he considered the ultimate order:

'BATTLE SPEED!'

With an effortless energy, the warship rapidly accelerated. On reaching the correct velocity, the vessel appeared to dissolve into an ethereal cloud of cosmic dust as it powered its way through the time-space continuum.

Deciding Mercer needed distracting, Osborn indicated the transceiver. 'Would you like to listen?' she said, sliding an earpiece towards him. 'At the moment it's mainly gossip from merchants passing through the Twelve Zones. It's best when the Terileptils are around. They're hysterical. A real hoot.'

Mercer inserted the device into his ear. 'Do you know what's being said?'

'I should hope so. Intergalactic transmission operators are required to speak a minimum of fifteen key languages. And with an on-board computer capable of translating a further hundred, we can cover most situations.'

Mercer was impressed. 'Dazzle me some more,' he said, almost flirting. 'For example, if a warship were about to attack, what would I hear in my earpiece?'

Osborn smiled. 'Probably nothing. Warships hunt using stealth or cloaking-devices. The only way it could be detected is by the deep-space scanner.'

Mercer nodded agreement.

'Look,' she continued, 'I've heard about what you've been saying. If being attacked really does worry you, remember the only ship we ever see is our own supply vessel. Believe me, no one is interested in us.'

But Ensign Osborn was mistaken.

Deep in the massive void of space, an immense warship changed course. Lytton, the vessel's commander, was using old-style diversion techniques to confuse observers as to his destination. Once the manoeuvres had been completed, and the course reset, the massive engines were set to maximum acceleration.

Now travelling at warp speed, unknown to Osborn, the battlecruiser was heading directly towards the *Vipod Mor*. Neither did she know that, when the cruiser arrived, there would be a terrible battle, followed by a visitation from the worst house guests in the universe ...

On board the TARDIS, the Doctor's mood had grown more cheerful. With the console reassembled and the ship's controls almost back on line, the Doctor was able to calculate their precise destination.

'Butler's Wharf,' he said brightly. 'Once the largest tea warehouse in the world.'

'Not being much of a tea drinker,' muttered Tegan, 'I just want to know how safe is the place?'

'How dangerous can a derelict Victorian warehouse be?' The Doctor smiled. He might have felt less optimistic if he had known that twenty people had been murdered in Shad Thames that morning. That several Second World War high-explosive aerial bombs might be lodged in the basement of the warehouse. And that two armed killers, dressed as London policemen patrolled the immediate area of the warehouse.

On the bunkbed that was her private space aboard the *Vipod Mor*, Ensign Fabian Osborn furtively took out her electronic journal, pressed it against the left temple of her head and started to think.

Entry

Time/Date Stella Sequence: Alpha18.7 Omega 9

I am annoyed ... no, **furious**.

Things are missing. Tools have disappeared.

No replacements possible

No little shop of horror around corner. No supply vessel to drop off replacements.

That's why zero theft on board Facility.

Agreement: people do not steal.

Yet tool box violated.

Pipe wrench, pliers, screwdriver gone.

I want them back.

NOW!

End of Entry

'So it goes ...'

Kurt Vonnegut Jr, a great American writer, wrote 'So it goes' over 100 times in his novel Slaughterhouse-5.

In the control room, the Officer-of-the-Watch, Lieutenant Tyler Mercer, was struggling to stay awake. Having spent two weeks in deep-space stasis, he was finding it difficult to re-establish his natural pattern of sleep.

Mercer half-watched Osborn and Seaton as they played chess. Such was their rapport and general sense of fun, it made Mercer wonder whether their relationship went further than that of fellow junior officers.

Suddenly Osborn unfolded her beautiful smile and said quietly: 'Check.' Her voice was now even softer. 'Mate in three moves.'

Seaton was gobsmacked – he couldn't believe it. Two PhDs, dozens of games played at professional level and she had 'checked' him in eight moves.

And he didn't see it coming!

Not a glimpse.

Not the smallest peek.

Seaton made a despairing noise. Suddenly Ensign Osborn had become intellectually interesting, he thought. Soon he and she would play a more intimate and exuberant game, something that would lead to a heightened state of deep understanding.

But not yet.

First, they had to deal with the high-pitched siren that had started to emanate from the deep-space scanner.

'I don't wanna rain on anyone's parade,' said Seaton, nonchalantly flicking a few computer buttons, 'but a battlecruiser has just entered the Facility's Exclusion Zone.'

Now fully awake, Mercer checked the readouts. Establishing the cruiser's ETA and lack of radio contact, he ordered a stage one alert. He also asked that the Captain be informed.

Osborn cleared her throat. 'Obviously no one told you, but since breakfast the Captain has … well … been *unavailable*. It's a case of too much Voxnic with too few cornflakes.'

'He's drunk?'

She nodded. 'It also means you are no longer Officer-of-the-Watch, but … acting Captain.'

The thought horrified Mercer. He was certainly hot for promotion, but not with a hostile warship heading towards him at warp speed, a defence system that was erratic to say the least and the undoubted piquancy of a drunken Captain lolling all over his first command.

'Show me the Orders of Engagement,' Mercer demanded. 'I need to know what I'm allowed to do.'

Moments later, the document was displayed on the large computer screen and, in spite of being highly complex, Osborn was able to speed-read it. Much to the team's surprise the Orders stated that an Officer-of-the-Watch, or acting Captain, would be allowed to repulse incoming hostiles using all defence systems at their disposal. That should have been good news, but, as Mercer already knew, the *Vipod Mor*'s defences were in a very fragile condition.

Reluctantly, Mercer asked the inevitable question: 'What do we actually have in the way of firepower?'

Again, Osborn downloaded the information, but the answer wasn't optimistic. Three laser cannons at full power. Two at fifty per cent and seven out of commission. All the torpedoes, both Bastick and high explosive, were non-functioning except for those on board the Starfighters. Deflector shields were at half power and the general condition of the mechanical transducers was poor.

'How many peashooters do we have?' muttered Seaton, without the slightest hint of irony.

Playfully, Osborn popped out her tongue. 'Don't listen to him,' she said. 'He forgets we still have two Starfighters.'

The F19 Mk9 Starfighter was considered one of the most powerful and deadliest ever built. With enormous firepower, it was capable of outmanoeuvring and destroying every battle weapon in the Twelve Galaxies. Although Mercer realised two fighters weren't that many, they could still be enough to give him the edge over the battlecruiser.

Suddenly Mercer felt he was back in control of the situation. He also realised that with a successful defence of the *Vipod Mor*, his permanent promotion to Captain could be only a few hours away.

For the first time in days, he experienced a real sense of wellbeing.

That was, until the battlecruiser decelerated from warp speed.

Now visible to the naked eye, it was possible to see that the unidentified vessel was a supercharged class six battlecruiser with a full complement of Grade A Terror Weapons with treble reinforced shields. Known in the military world as the Ball Crusher, it was a highly dangerous killing machine which had been massively modified by the Daleks.

'Do we surrender now?' enquired Seaton, still without irony.

'To lose the Facility without a fight might be seen as cowardly,' Mercer mumbled. 'To make a stand against a vessel that could instantly destroy us could be deemed a hideous mistake. But to throw away our lives without trying to defend ourselves would be a pointless waste.'

Osborn was confused. 'I'm sure that's great rhetoric,' she said, 'but what do we do in the real world?'

Suddenly Mercer's indecision was gone. 'Go to red alert,' he ordered. 'Scramble the Starfighters. And send out an under-attack emergency signal.'

As the siren echoed throughout the *Vipod Mor*, the crew emerged from their various resting places. With little enthusiasm, they ambled towards their different defence zones. Many, believing it to be only a practice alert, were without helmets, gasmasks and even weapons. For Mercer, it was horrifying to watch trained marines perform in such a sloppy and uncharacteristic manner.

'*THIS IS NOT A DRILL!*' bellowed Mercer over the public address. 'WE ARE IN FULL DEFENSIVE MODE!'

In deep space, a mere forty minutes from the *Vipod Mor*, the two Starfighters, their engines racing at full power, were locked onto the battlecruiser. With Bastick torpedoes primed, the fighters opened fire and, like a swarm of angry hornets, the grouped missiles hurtled towards the cruiser. Igniting superchargers, the fighters turned and powered their way from the missiles' impending back-blast,

But instead of instant destruction, the cruiser's protective force shield absorbed the massive impact. Turning to attack again, the fighters fired yet more torpedoes followed by several savage broadsides of laser cannon that nothing should have survived … but still the cruiser remained undamaged.

As the two fighters turned in a vast arc to attack from a higher, deadlier vector, a sudden flash of intense light was launched from the cruiser. Enveloping them, the mixture of combined light and starfighters swirled as though being mashed inside a massive centrifuge.

A few seconds later there was an enormous explosion and the Starfighters vaporised …

Mercer switched off the klaxon. Strangely, the sudden lack of noise seemed piercingly loud. He was truly stunned by events.

Osborn was on the verge of tears. 'Even a modified class six battlecruiser cannot shoot down two Starfighters that quickly,' she said. 'Certainly not in a single sortie. It simply doesn't have the weapons, shield power or even speed of response.'

'This one does,' muttered Seaton. 'This one is a killer.'

As a rule, Mercer didn't like war machines being rated over and beyond the craft's prescribed capabilities. Yet he could not deny the battlecruiser had emerged from nowhere, not been observed until at the very fringe of the *Vipod Mor*'s exclusion zone and had leisurely shot down two Starfighters.

Mercer was even less happy when told the battlecruiser was now scanning the Facility's power generators. That usually meant someone was going to attack.

With computers switched to defence mode, shields in place and airlocks sealed, Seaton pressed the Master Control, but instead of a full set of clearance lights, a cluster of warning ones danced across a screen. 'Airlock Three has not sealed.'

'Alert maintenance,' ordered Mercer. 'I want a full repair team in place *now*.'

Seaton worked swiftly and positive things started to happen.

'Have ordnance set-up laser cannon teams around the entrance of Airlock Three,' ordered Mercer. 'Nothing must get in!'

Although he had secured the Facility, he knew there was something missing, something that would help defend the *Vipod Mor*.

But what?

The river slapped and sloshed against the unloading piers! of Butler's Wharf. The water was dark and swirled with the waste and debris of human life. Known as the River Thames, it had existed forever.

The Celts called it Tamesas, the Romans Tamesis. The name probably means 'dark', not dark as in hue, but dark as in an unfriendly place where evil spirits steal the lives of unwary swimmers.

Chapter Four

As the Thames continued to slurp and slap, a harsh scraping sound, like a scrapyard being turned over by a massive earthmover, could be heard. This was followed by a blinking white light beginning to form on the main peer outside Butler's Wharf. As it grew brighter, the blue outline of an obsolete, metropolitan police box appeared, then faded, then appeared again …

Finally, everything stopped,
became silent.
Neatly parked, The TARDIS was
back on Earth.

Now here's a thing …

No one seemed to understand why seats had not been built into the TARDIS. Even car ones, fitted with safety belts, would be more comfortable than bouncing around the floor of the console room. What was annoying was that whenever seats came up for discussion, the Doctor would disappear. It was as though he didn't want people to get too comfortable, and maybe think of the TARDIS as a permanent home.

Not today, nor any other.

Now fully materialised, the door of the time machine was opened and the Doctor and his companions tumbled out.

'And here we are,' said the Doctor. 'Butler's Wharf, our destination.'

Alongside it, spanning the Thames, was Tower Bridge. Known as a bascule, the bridge's two independent rising leaves opened to allow sailing ships to pass through. When first built it was the largest bascule of its kind.

'Neat bridge,' said Tegan.

'Yes,' said the Doctor enthusiastically. 'Originally powered by steam and completed around 1894.'

'Fascinating,' said Tegan joylessly.

'It is,' insisted the Doctor. 'The bridge was constructed from 11,000 tons of steel and its piers contain over 70,000 tons of concrete. The cladding was created from Cornish granite and Portland stone.'

'Despite the stone stuff, it's still a neat bridge,' muttered Tegan.

The Doctor ignored her. 'I first recommended Portland to Inigo Jones who, at the time, was building a restaurant or something, somewhere. I then suggested it to Christopher.'

'Christopher Robin?' Turlough inquired languidly.

'*Actually*, it was Christopher Wren. When he was building that little church.'

'Didn't we meet him?' said Tegan.

The Doctor nodded. 'That's right, when we were here for the Great Fire of London.'

'Oh, yeah,' she said remembering. 'Those Terileptil things were around.'

'And do you remember the Globe? How we met Will and I gave him the title for his latest play. I think it was "The Importance of Being Earnest".'

'That was Oscar Wilde,' jeered Turlough.

'Yes, well. I knew him too.' A little embarrassed, the Time Lord said. 'I think we should get on.'

'Yeah, well, so this is 1984, eh?' said Tegan, passing a critical eye over the dereliction that was Butler's Wharf. 'This isn't how I remember London. My one was Earl's Court for living, Knightsbridge for shopping and the King's Road for fun.'

The Doctor huffed-and-puffed a little. 'What you're looking at may be a little derelict, but you are standing at the heart of what was one of the largest ports on the planet Earth.'

'This Australian doesn't really do colonial history.'

'You might learn something,' snapped Turlough. 'Read a book or try watching a documentary. The TARDIS library is full of them.'

Tegan didn't like being reprimanded, especially by someone as youthful, irritating and precocious as Turlough.

'It's all right for you,' she shouted, 'but I haven't benefited from some posh, public school.'

Turlough shuddered at the thought of his old *alma mater*. To him, Brendon was an institute for little more than modern-day thuggery, where young boys were abused and teachers sadistically caned students for the slightest of reasons.

'Enough squabbling.' The Doctor removed a small electronic instrument from his pocket. 'We need to concentrate on finding the entrance to the time corridor.'

Switching on the device, it automatically flicked through a series of images until locating a diagrammatic representation of Shad Thames. Pressing another switch, the image was projected onto a nearby wall. 'That alley,' the Doctor said, pointing at a long, squiggly line on the map, 'leads to a service road where some of the warehouse entrances are located.' Then, as though to add authority to his statement, he jabbed energetically at the projected image. 'That is where we start to look.'

Tegan stared at the map. 'Can't we use the TARDIS to search for the time corridor?'

The Doctor shook his head. 'Normally I would, but there's too much time-drag affecting the instrumentation. It's too dangerous. Could finish up materialising inside a wall.'

Followed by his reluctant companions, the Doctor strode off down the alley, past the derelict Custom Houses, with their spooky atmosphere, and into a side road of Shad Thames. Suddenly the Doctor made an abrupt left turn. 'Along here,' he said. 'And we need to hurry.' Almost magically, like a two-headed sangorstyk being chased by a hungry speelsnape, the Time Lord doubled his speed.

'Hang on,' Tegan called. 'I'm wearing heels.'

The Time Lord, his face taut, screeched to a halt. 'Listen very carefully,' he said firmly, 'if we don't close the time corridor very soon, innocent people could die.'

He was right. But little did the Doctor know that, elsewhere, the killing had already started ...

Without warning, a low-impact torpedo (LIT) ripped into the Facility's superstructure, killing all but two of the medical crew.

The LIT, also known as the 'sneak', created havoc by 'sneaking' in, causing maximum damage to the crew and then 'sneaking' out leaving the structure of the ship relatively undamaged.

Since the LIT was a re-usable weapon, during a highly confused period of the planet's history, the Earth Protection Agency had accidentally granted an environment award to be given jointly to LIT and the Intergalactic Federation of Jam & Marmalade Manufacturers.

Because of a bumper crop, the Federation had decided to 'sneak' extra fruit into their jams and marmalades. They then smeared a million units of advertising over everything and, somehow, the two campaigns became conjoined. As a consequence of this confusion, where weapons of war should have gone, jam and marmalade arrived and where jam was required, weapons of war were delivered. The oddest thing of all was that after eating so much of the conserve, more people died of obesity than from the effects of the LIT.

Or so the story went, especially when told in the Voxnic Bars up and down Solar System 82.

In the control room of the *Vipod Mor,* sitting in front of a computer, Osborn was attempting to nurse back to life some of the Facility's torpedoes. Although her maths was correct, the Siddion Quartz? batteries that powered the killing machines had been discharged too long for them ever again to hold a charge or function properly.

Elsewhere, in the control room, Mercer stared at the only security screen still capable of showing Airlock Three. Despite a dozen engineers at work, the airlock remained stubbornly open. Even if closed, Mercer had decided, hostile Troopers could easily overrun the Facility as the airlock was too big to effectively defend.

Mercer continued to stare at the screen as though hoping its circuitry might contain the answer to his problem. At first it didn't, but then, after a little while, words came to him …

Bulwark, which he didn't fully understand.

Redoubt, which seemed a very old-fashioned word.

Then there it was:

'Barricades!' Mercer said out loud. 'We need barricades.'

Seaton, who was busily calculating the vector and speed of the cruiser, was surprised by Mercer's abrupt remark. 'Barricades?' Seaton smiled broadly. 'Last time I looked, the store was fresh out.'

'Then we construct our own.' Mercer was now bubbling with excitement. 'Use anything available – chairs, tables, boxes. Stuff that can be stacked to create a low strong wall. Make a dozen of them. As many as suitable materials will allow.'

'You're planning to fight, eh?' Seaton was unsure whether the thought made him feel brave or afraid.

'We have little choice,' said Mercer pointing at the computer screen. 'Your own calculations say the battlecruiser is positioned to destroy us.'

And as though to make a rather unpleasant point, another torpedo ripped into the *Vipod Mor*'s superstructure and yet more crew members died.

On the bridge of the battlecruiser, Commander Gustav Lytton studied the performance of his LITs. With the *Vipod Mor*'s water-making machinery gone and its general defences much reduced, it was only a matter of time before Lytton completed his mission.

Deeply focused on his battle plan, Lytton didn't hear the Supreme Dalek glide onto the bridge. Looking larger than the average combat Dalek, its black body and white nodules made it appear highly authoritative.

Which of course it was.

'Your plan succeeds?' the Supreme Dalek oozed.

Lytton smiled stiffly. He had worked with Daleks before. Usually he found them noisy, aggressive and highly repetitive, but this one was different. It was more reflective, quieter and, as it would turn out, far more dangerous. It also appeared to know what others were thinking, often before they did. He bowed his head. 'My plan goes well, Supreme Dalek.'

The Dalek silently crossed the bridge and peered at a row of screens. 'There is an urgent change of plan,' it said.

Lytton looked surprised.

'The *Vipod Mor* has informed Star Fleet Base that it is under attack.' There was a slight hint of rant caressing the edge of his voice. 'The crew and the *Vipod Mor* are to be destroyed. There will be no survivors.'

Now that sounded more like an old-school Dalek.

'What about the Prisoner?' asked Lytton.

'He must not be harmed. He will be rescued as ordered.'

Realising it would be a waste of time to argue, Lytton simply bowed his head as a mark of respect. 'May I ask why you want the Prisoner alive?'

'You may,' said the Supreme Dalek, 'but only a fool would expect an answer.'

Lytton swayed slightly. The moment was to be savoured. After all it wasn't often you heard a Dalek trying to be witty.

At Shad Thames, in the basement of the warehouse, tea had been drunk and sandwiches eaten. To make the area more comfortable, a large heavy canvas curtain had been drawn across the end of the cellar creating a much-improved sense of cosiness. Everyone seemed content, but that wasn't entirely true.

Professor Sarah Laird, an expert in metallurgy, had spent two days trying to find the fuse compartment on what were possibly several Second World War aerial bombs. She had searched every centimetre of the cylinders, but found nothing. She had then applied every known test to determine the base metal used in the cylinder's manufacture, but the results proved negative.

Sergeant Graham Calder had managed explosive devices from every war in the last one hundred and seventy years. He had even defused an ancient piece of ordnance from the American Civil War. As with others, he brought a vast amount of knowledge to the situation, but couldn't provide any real answers concerning the cylinders.

Colonel Patrick Archer was the academic, recruited as an expert in everything theoretical concerning explosives. Yet, like the others, he was beginning to wonder how he could justify his presence on site.

Feeling totally frustrated, the trio were on the verge of giving up. Yet in spite of being unable to identify the cylinders' metal content, there was still one question they had refused to ask out loud – were the cylinders from another planet? In 1984, to trained scientists, the answer had to be 'no'.

With the barricades under construction, Seaton and Osborn, watched by Mercer, were trying to discover the on-board frequency being used by the battlecruiser. Knowing what a warship is saying to itself is always useful in a fight, but the commander of this ship was too clever to be caught so easily.

Instead, and purely by chance, they discovered the ship had entered a semi-conducted arc. This made the cruiser appear it was about to connect at Airlock One when it was really Airlock Three.

Mercer was concerned. 'How long before they dock?'

'With time stretch compensation …' Seaton ran his tongue over a dry bottom lip in mock concentration, 'maybe around seventeen minutes.'

Almost involuntarily Mercer fingered a small bulge under his tunic top. 'I've a special commission for you, Osborn' he said producing an electronic key.

Osborn eyed it suspiciously.

'This is important,' said Mercer. 'Should the Facility's defences completely fail …' He paused almost melodramatically … 'If it fails, you will destroy the Prisoner.' Mercer thrust the key into Osborn's hands. 'Are you up to it?'

Osborn shrugged. She didn't like the prospect of killing someone, or finishing up on trial in an Intergalactic Court on the fringe of some half-forgotten star system. Worse still, she didn't like the idea of being accused of murder, or spending thirty years in a tinclavic mine as the appetiser to a bunch of drunken Terileptils.

Turning the key over in her hand, the device looked more suited to a medieval castle than a prison cell on board a spacecraft. 'OK,' she said reluctantly, 'I should be able do that.'

Mercer nodded his approval. 'I'll be at Airlock Three,' he said. 'I can be of more use there.'

As he started to leave, Seaton called: 'What about me?'

Mercer didn't stop walking. Instead he half turned and said over his shoulder: 'Go with Osborn. She might like the back-up.'

It had started to rain again.

This time it was the fine stuff. The sort that makes you feel wet and nasty.

With slicing arm movements, the Doctor scythed his way along Shad Thames. Fortunately, the pavement, being free of pedestrians, allowed his progress to be safe, speedy and uninhibited. Doing their best to keep up, Tegan and Turlough, jogged painfully behind.

Suddenly the Time Lord skidded to a halt beside the door to a warehouse.

The next moment, that door swung open and, from the gloom, a hand grabbed the Time Lord's arm.

'D-d-don't come in here. S-s-soldiers!' The voice was strained and agitated and belonged to Quartermaster Sergeant Raymond Arthur Stien. 'It's highly dangerous!' he added urgently. As Stien tried to convince the Doctor, he suddenly lost his balance and collapsed. Quickly, the Doctor examined him and guessed he had fainted from a lack of food.

'Nothing a good meal won't cure,' said the Time Lord. 'That and a good bath.'

'Forget the washing,' said Tegan. 'Look how this joker is dressed.'

The Time Lord fingered the collar of Stien's tunic. 'It isn't from Earth.'

'It's made from Polytine,' Turlough interrupted. 'Usually worn by the military. He must have come down the time corridor.'

Suddenly there was a groan – Stien was waking up. 'You must h-h-help me,' he said. 'I am so hungry.'

Rummaging in his pocket the Doctor produced the last of his jelly babies and offered them to Stien. With a happy grin, he quickly devoured them. 'Thank you,' he said. 'Very tasty.'

'If you tell me who is operating the time corridor I'll get you more to eat.'

In a nanosecond Stien's expression turned from happy to deeply sad. 'I don't know,' he said.

'But you travelled with others?'

Stien shrugged.

'Then where were they from?'

'All over the place, but they w-w-weren't all from the same period.'

The Doctor looked concerned. 'We must find out who's behind this.'

'No!' Stien was again terrified. 'There are real soldiers in the warehouse. M-m-men who kill.'

The Doctor smiled, his expression that of mock bravery. 'Then maybe they can tell us what's going on.'

Without hesitating, the Time Lord pulled Stien onto his feet and urged him into the warehouse. Then with promises of 'real' food, he persuaded him to the top of the first stairway and into the warehouse area. Although Stien was now cooperating, and had shown the Doctor approximately where the portal had been, the actual entrance remained elusive.

Unimpressed by Stien's performance Tegan and Turlough had started to search other areas of the storage room.

'Dark ... isn't it?' muttered Turlough, poking at something with the toe of his shoe.

Tegan wasn't listening. Instead she had been trying not to ruin her stockings by crawling around the filthy floor. 'Look, Doctor,' she called, holding up several metal objects. 'Cartridge cases ...' She sniffed them. 'And recently fired.'

The Doctor looked at the casings and declared they had been used in a machine pistol.

'That's not very alien.'

'Why advertise who you are?'

Tegan was perplexed. 'They brought a great big time corridor with them,' she said with a little more incredulity than intended. 'I mean, how much more obvious can you actually be?'

Chapter Five

Under Mercer's supervision, large boxes had been found, loaded with various types of ballast and then carefully stacked. Office tables had been hauled into use, heavy armchairs rescued from rest areas and dragged into duty. Steel mesh was discovered and woven around the furniture for extra strength. Load-moving vehicles, commandeered from the *Vipod*'s warehouse, had been driven to the airlock, parked and then disabled. Everything was going well until there was a mighty explosion. A LIT had hit one of the electrical sub-stations. This not only caused a massive power failure, but created thick acrid smoke that spread along the corridors and into the ducting.

'We should surrender,' said a crewmember. 'We can't fight. We don't even have an effective deflector shield.'

*

Elsewhere, on board, there was another female crewmember with a wildly pungent view. Dr Elizabeth Styles, accompanied by her damaged robot nurse, made their way along the corridor, into Airlock Three and directly to where Mercer was standing. 'The Captain is dead,' she bellowed directly into Mercer's face. 'And the west wing has taken a direct hit.'

Styles extended her right hand towards Monda, her nurse robot. 'On our way here, Ordnance gave me this.' Monda placed a small satchel onto Styles's open hand. 'They said you would know what to do with it.'

Carefully, Mercer examined the bag for a moment and then gently eased it open. Inside was an anti-personnel mine capable of creating an enormous amount of damage. Behind the satchel's fastening was a three-second fuse.

A Three-Second Fuse!

Once triggered, the leave-taking of whoever used it could be a brief and incredibly messy affair. As Mercer cogitated the murderous reality of a bomb without a proper fuse, the words …

'*Found them …*' echoed around Airlock Three.

Waving a pipe wrench and a large pair of pliers above her head, one of the engineers stood frozen faced. 'Osborn's been looking for these. They were rammed in the door opening mechanism,' she shouted. Instead of a congratulatory cheer from the other engineers, there was nothing, except a thoughtful, pragmatic silence. Pliers and pipe wrenches, everyone was thinking, do not find their own way into a door mechanism, that is, not without serious help.

The news was bad – a saboteur was on board. It could've been anyone. The person on shift with you. Someone telling you a joke. Wanting to be your friend.

Suddenly there was another noise …

BOOM!

… echoing and rebounding around the *Vipod Mor*.

BOOM!

… it went again.

Although no one had heard the sound before, everyone knew what was making it.

BOOM!

The battlecruiser was trying to dock alongside the *Vipod Mor*.

Then a terrible *CRUNCH* as clamps from the battlecruiser locked the two vessels tightly together.

The Battle for the *Vipod Mor* was almost over.

Urged on by Mercer, the crew threw themselves at the massive sheet of case-hardened tinclavic that protected the outer airlock. With a lot of pulling, cursing and straining, it slowly began to move. A few minutes later the plate was in place and the airlock sealed.

'Take cover,' shouted Mercer. 'We must remain focused!' Quickly the crew took their places behind the various sections of prefabricated barricades. While Mercer checked the crew's positioning, he couldn't help but notice how many of them were still without gas masks, hard helmets and even weapons.

'Would you like me to prime that thing?' said Dr Styles, pointing at the black satchel Mercer was still holding.

'Can you?'

Styles grunted. 'Maybe you don't know,' she said firmly, 'but I was a soldier before I trained to be a doctor.'

Removing a lint bandage from her breast pocket, Styles attached one end of it to the three-second fuse and then wedged the anti-personnel device in a cavity by the outer entrance to Airlock Three. Unreeling the bandage, she manipulated it back to behind one of the makeshift barricades. All it needed was a simple tug and the satchel would cause serious annihilation.

Outside the door of the control room, a LIT off-loaded its torpedo which then exploded and almost blew Osborn and Seaton off their feet.

Seaton looked at her. 'Time to deal with the Prisoner.'

Making their way to the far end of the control room, they opened a small, wooden cupboard containing an ancient-looking safe. On the front of the safe's door was a push-button combination lock with a full alphabet, a set of numerals and an extensive selection of mathematical symbols. Inside the safe was the control mechanism of the device that would destroy the Prisoner.

To open the safe required a letter and symbol group consisting of eighteen separate digits. Given the complexity of the grouping, it was difficult to insert the password without making an error. This was made even worse as, once inside the safe, there was a large biscuit-like tin fitted with yet another combination and a twelve-centimetre slit designed to take the electronic key. Such was the complexity of the key the slightest scratch would render its performance useless.

At Airlock Three, most of the crew were crouched behind their barricades …

Some prayed.

Others waited for the inevitable …

Some thought about family, friends or a lover …

All wished they were somewhere else.

Dr Styles, now much calmer, sat next to Mercer. With her laser sidearm resting in her lap, the gas mask around her neck and the end of her detonator bandage clutched firmly in her hand, she was ready for action … or at least she hoped she was. Nearby stood Monda, upright and erect, more a waiting bodyguard than a damaged robot nurse.

Behind another of the barricades was the laser cannon, its murderous muzzle pointing deep into Airlock Three, its firing mechanism primed and the ammunition chamber fully loaded.

The wait continued …

It was a now a full hour since the cruiser had locked on to the *Vipod Mor*. Although there had been some activity, the airlock area was now quiet. Even with monitoring radio frequencies, nothing had been heard. The one certain thing they had learned about the aggressor was they knew how to wait quietly …

Suddenly there was a scratching sound.

A rat?

A space louse?

Something *evil*?

But what appeared was a splendid example of *Felis catus*, in this case known as Sir Runcible, the Facility's cat. He was completely black, his girth impressive and his name a reminder of the ancient Edward Lear poem.

Oblivious of what was happening, the cat ran out of the airlock – a favourite haunt, where the juiciest rats could be chased – and jumped up onto one of the makeshift barricades and stretched out its long, sleek body. Sir Runcible then started to roll around clawing at the air. Tiring of that, he chased his tail in an assortment of sharp, sudden moves. With the tension gone, the crew started to laugh at the animal's antics.

Concerned they would lose concentration, Mercer ordered they should check settings and power levels on their laser rifles. The weapons clicked and clacked as they were prepared for action. 'We may only get one chance to destroy the hostiles,' said Mercer. 'Check your weapons are set to kill.'

With the crew refocused, the cat realised he had lost his audience. With a last look round at those who fed him, he ran off at a speed more suited to a greyhound. No sooner had he gone than there was a sudden crash from behind Airlock Three, followed by a huge explosion. As the airlock's protective plate collapsed, it revealed a wall of grey metal in waiting: a phalanx of Daleks, ready to administer death.

With most of the lighting gone, and the area thick with smoke, the Daleks looked like a ghostly horde emerging through a shroud of death. With their manipulator arms appearing to sniff the air and their all-powerful guns focused on Mercer and the remaining crew in the redoubt, everyone seemed to be waiting.

Then suddenly came the screech, the hideous sound that had sent fear roaring across the universe for endless generations –

EXTERMINATE! EXTERMINATE! EXTERMINATE!

To which there could only be one reply:

'*OPEN FIRE!*' Mercer yelled.

His forces obeyed in a unified single assault: every weapon fired, sending a hail of shrapnel, laser fire and even a dozen steel arrows from a sporting longbow, tearing into the Daleks' body casings. For a full two minutes there was a terrible exchange of fire causing Daleks to explode and killing crew members. Desperate to get the upper hand, Mercer ordered Styles to operate her anti-personnel mine. This she did and destroyed a further fifteen Daleks. Much to everyone's relief, the firepower from the *Vipod Mor* was proving greater and more effective than expected, and Mercer's barricades had proved a work of inspiration.

In spite of all this, casualties were high. Valuable and vital members of the crew were destroyed. Even Monda, the nurse robot, was finally brought down. Fighting like a warrior, she had protected Dr Styles during several bouts of vicious conflict. It was extraordinary to see her perform, like a gifted gymnast, protecting her closest friend.

It was a sad loss, as were the untimely deaths of many fine crew members.

*

Aboard the Dalek ship, a grim-faced Lytton watched events unfold on his security screen. 'I told you this would happen,' he said. 'They mined the corridor.'

There was a long pause. Then sounding as though it had just been out for a heavy lunch, the Supreme Dalek gave what sounded like a loud belch. 'The attack must continue,' it rasped. 'The glory of the Daleks must be celebrated.'

'Celebrated – they almost wiped you out. The *Vipod Mor*'s position has proven too strong. Your battle tactics won't succeed. Not unless,' Lytton urged, 'you use ZP gas.'

The Dalek swung round to face him. 'The Prisoner must not be harmed.'

Lytton was growing tired of the Dalek always stating the obvious. 'My Troopers will follow through the gas attack, snatch the Prisoner and bring him directly to our medical facilities.'

The Dalek didn't reply. In spite of being in the middle of a serious sortie, while trying to discuss tactics, the Supreme Dalek's focus seemed to be elsewhere.

'I hope I'm not interrupting, Supreme Dalek?' Lytton's tone was almost rude. 'Did you hear what I said?'

Suddenly the Dalek seemed to regain concentration and snapped back into focus. 'I have considered your request. You will use the gas. You will succeed.'

Although far from heartfelt, Lytton gave a small nod of appreciation. 'You will not be disappointed, Supreme Dalek.'

Another grunt came from the Dalek. 'If you fail, you will be …' But instead of the immortal word, the combination of letters that terrified a universe faded, leaving the remaining syllables unformed and incomplete.

The Supreme Dalek turned to leave the bridge. 'The Doctor, the arch enemy of the Daleks, is our prisoner on Earth. A Dalek has been dispatched to bring him to our battlecruiser. When he arrives you will be responsible for his custody.'

'I know,' said Lytton sarcastically. 'If he escapes, I will die.'

'It will be worse. You will remain conscious, in a cryo chamber forever. You will never sleep. You will be permanently awake!'

Lytton watched as the Supreme Dalek left the bridge. He couldn't believe what he had heard. Earlier a *witty* Supreme Dalek, now an *ironic* one. Should this continue, he thought, how much longer would it be before there was an all-singing, all-dancing one?

Turlough sat on the edge of a broken tea chest and watched Stien shuffle around the room. 'What exactly are you looking for?'

'The remains of Galloway,' came the morose reply.

Turlough shrugged. 'And he is?'

Stien looked even sadder. 'He helped me escape. They k-k-k-killed him.' He pointed at the floor. 'It must have been somewhere here.' Stien was now on the verge of tears.

'Don't mope,' said Turlough. 'Celebrate you are still alive.'

But Stien was too sad for that.

Tired of talking, and even more fed up with Stien's whining, Turlough wandered deeper into the warehouse. Surprised by how quickly it had become darker, Turlough took out a torch, switched it on and saw he was standing alongside two tea chests, newer and better preserved than many others around. He bent to see what was written on their sides. As he did, he found himself tumbling and rolling in a void that was without resistance, friction or possibly even air.

Without air?

This made Turlough wonder how he was still alive.

Welcome to the time corridor, Turlough thought. *So, this is how I die.* He lost his nerve and started to scream.

'Doctor! Doctor! Help me!'

Although Tegan didn't hear the actual words, she *sensed* the scream as it swirled its way along the time corridor.

'DO ... C ... TOR!' The voice was even more distorted.

'Didn't you feel that?' said Tegan pointing to a corner of the storage area. 'I'm sure it was from over there.'

'It's too late,' groaned Stien. 'Most likely the t-t-t-time corridor has taken him.'

'Don't worry.' The Doctor was again trying to sound ultra-cool. 'If it has, we'll get him back.' Then as though to prove the point, he picked up a length of wood and slashed at the air to test its strength.

'Galloway d-d-did the stick thing,' said Stien, sounding like the living embodiment of doom. 'Then they killed him.'

'Don't worry,' said the Doctor. 'I won't let that happen again.'

Although Turlough wasn't Tegan's best friend, she was genuinely concerned something really bad might have happened to him. 'You really think he fell into the time corridor, Doctor?'

'Anything is possible where Turlough is concerned.' The Time Lord thrust his stick into a pile of rubbish. 'Even him hiding under this.'

Tegan smiled. 'I could look for him downstairs.'

'I'd rather you didn't wander off.' The Doctor was adamant. 'You'd be safer calling him.'

Sergeant Calder, who had just opened his toolbox, was the first to hear the voice. Colonel Archer, who was reading the *Guardian*, nodded – he had heard the voice, too. Carefully he folded his newspaper and placed it on the table. As Calder and Archer strapped on their sidearms, the lance corporal took down his weapon from the security rack and then opened the canvas curtain. Ordering Professor Laird and the second soldier to wait in the cellar, the others started to climb the stairs.

'TURLOUGH...'

Occasionally thrusting at piles of rubbish with his stick, the Doctor continued to search the first floor of the warehouse.

'It was definitely here,' said Stien, pointing. 'Right there. Exactly w-w-w-where you're standing.'

The Doctor looked at the floor, but couldn't see anything.

'Trust me,' said Stien. 'Where you're standing is the entrance to the time corridor.'

As he spoke, a small squad of soldiers entered. Seeing they were armed, the Doctor stopped his search and, in a conciliatory manner, placed his stick carefully on the floor. 'How do you do?' said the Time Lord, smiling broadly. 'I'm the Doctor. Over there is Mr Stien. And slouching in the corner is Tegan Jovanka, an Australian.'

'Thanks, Doc,' Tegan muttered.

'I'm Major Archer, acting Colonel on attachment to the Bomb Squad. Over there is my Sergeant, Calder. Not only does he make an excellent pot of tea, but he is also a superb shot.'

The Doctor smiled amiably, though he was unsure as to how the pot of tea fitted into the threat.

'And you, sir,' said Archer turning to Stien. 'As we entered, I heard you mention something about an entrance to a time corridor?'

Stien turned ashen. He didn't know what to say

'As everyone here heard our conversation,' the Doctor interjected, 'it seems pointless to deny it. Allow me to bring you up to speed.'

He talked a little about time corridors.

He then talked about cylinders that looked like Second World War aerial bombs but didn't have fuses.

Finally he talked about alien objects in general, what would be considered, to the lay public of this place and time, *Scary stuff.*

Although he didn't know how much the Bomb Squad had already discovered, the Doctor found it gratifying that the mention of things alien didn't seem to perturb them. Even though Archer and his team were displaying a high degree of sensitivity, the Doctor decided not to mention the TARDIS. Untrained military fingers poking around in her delicate areas were something to avoid.

With a need to report what the Doctor had disclosed to his HQ, the Colonel ordered the field radio to be brought to him from the cellar. Moments later it arrived, carried by the second soldier and escorted by Professor Laird. Once she had been appraised of the Doctor's story, Laird told of her own experience the previous night.

Of how she had sensed someone lurking behind her.

That she saw a silhouette dissolve into the floor.

Suddenly Stien kicked into gear. 'Was he d-d-d-dressed in black?'

Laird nodded.

'They g-g-guard the time corridor,' continued Stien. 'They know all the entrances. That's why they can disappear so quickly.'

The Doctor didn't respond.

Something else was now distracting him.

Something in his subconscious.

Something three scoops away from an enormous disaster …

Then it happened.

The Dalek sent to collect the Doctor from Earth suddenly appeared. Whirring and roaring, it seemed to spiral out of the floor, a nasty, aggressive, discombobulated creature of vileness that lived to hate and loved to kill.

EXTERMINATE! EXTERMINATE! EXTERMINATE!

It screeched and screamed as though red-hot nails had been driven into its most sensitive parts.

'Take cover!' the Doctor shouted.

Archer signalled that his men should obey the command as they unholstered their sidearms and the soldiers flicked off their rifle safety catches.

'Is this thing with you?' Archer demanded.

The Doctor shook his head. 'Although it's not entirely unexpected.'

As he spoke, the Dalek opened fire and a soldier fell dead. Calder and Archer returned fire, but the bullets had little effect on the Dalek's extra-reinforced casing. 'Aim at the eyepiece,' shouted the Time Lord. 'The stalk on top of the dome!'

Quickly, and without hesitation, Archer, Calder and Miller opened fire. The Dalek's bulbous lens exploded, sending the creature into a paroxysm of rage.

'I CANNOT SEE! MY VISION IS IMPAIRED! I CANNOT SEE!'

The Dalek continued to scream as it circled wildly in an uncontrolled manner. Then, as though trying to escape from the warehouse, it hurled itself against the access door that was above Shad Thames. Seeing what was happening, the Doctor rushed forward and wrestled with the door's restraining bar.

On succeeding, and helped by Tegan, they threw the access doors open with a loud crash. Disturbed by the sudden noise, the startled Dalek blindly swung around catching Tegan a hard blow with what remained of its eyepiece. As she collapsed, Professor Laird dragged her out of harm's way, while Calder, Archer and the Doctor threw themselves against the flailing Dalek, sending it crashing into the street below. On impact, the Dalek exploded, launching a terrible rumble along the canyon-like streets.

Back in the warehouse the Doctor and Calder slammed and locked the access doors.

'Tegan needs an ambulance,' said Professor Laird urgently. 'We must get her to hospital.'

'I'm fine,' Tegan protested, trying to sit up – and promptly falling backwards.

While Calder tried to contact the ambulance service by field radio, Laird carried out basic first aid, applying a lint patch to the wound on her forehead. The Doctor, Archer and the lance corporal cleared away bits and pieces of the Dalek's casing. The Doctor then helped Laird take Tegan down to the camp bed in the basement.

On the Dalek ship, a confused Turlough stumbled out of the time corridor and into a reception area, feeling like the schoolboy he was dressed as. He tended to wear the reviled uniform in the hope that those the Doctor came up against would underestimate him, or even show pity for a lost child should he choose to put on that act. But here, with Daleks involved, he knew nothing would make any difference.

Slowly he made his way along a corridor and, not knowing where he was going, turned into a dark alcove. Searching around the walls, he found a pressure plate and pressed it. As a door slid silently open, Turlough, without hesitation, passed through to a dark smaller chamber behind the alcove. After allowing his eyes to adjust to the low lighting, he noticed shapes on the floor – *dead human beings!* These were the people killed in Shad Thames, although Turlough didn't know that at the time. In fear and disgust, he rushed from the room. Now on the verge of tears, he ran off along the corridor. What sort of new hell had he entered? More to the point, how could he get away from it?

Smoke hung over the razed remains of Airlock Three. It was impossible to believe that an ill-prepared ship led by an inexperienced officer could have caused so much damage

Dr Elizabeth Styles, still in place with Mercer behind a barricade, changed the prism in her laser before pressing home a fresh power pack. Out of habit, she switched on the safety. 'How long before they try again?' she muttered.

The reply came instantly as a barrage of laser fire poured into the barricade in front of her. Attempting to return fire, Styles and Mercer saw three battlecruiser Troopers, using semi-destroyed Dalek carcasses as cover, push several large white cylinders towards them.

'*Open fire!*' Mercer shouted.

Although the shooting was accurate, the Troopers still continued to advance.

'Grenades!' bellowed Mercer, but someone shouted back – 'We're out!'

That was when the panic started. It grew worse when the Troopers opened their cylinders and a smoke-like substance poured out.

'*Gas!*' Mercer was desperate now. 'Masks on!'

But, with the exception of Mercer and Styles, few of the crew had any protection. 'Run!' screamed Styles, but for some it was too late. Enveloped by the gas, people started to die. Internal organs atrophied or erupted like massive boils, causing bodies to rapidly decompose. The truly unlucky developed a form of accelerated leprosy where flesh and sinew instantly started to rot. Whoever had designed the gas seemed to possess a highly warped obsession with reducing organic living beings to little more than puddles of acrid slime.

Knowing they had to get away and to maximise their cover, Mercer and Styles crawled back to the control room on their hands and knees.

'It's over,' said Mercer. 'We can't fight this.' And he was right.

'So what can we do?' asked Styles.

'You won't like this,' he said tentatively, 'but the station has a self-destruct system.'

'It also has a bathroom,' snapped Styles, 'so what's your point?'

Mercer paused. 'Well,' he said, 'we can operate the self-destruct.'

Styles wasn't impressed. 'Can't we use the bath instead?'

'No water.'

'So, as an alternative, we commit suicide?'

Mercer shrugged. 'Sorry,' he said, 'but it's better than a second date with me.'

Further up the corridor, Lytton and his Elite Guard entered Airlock Three. Having checked all crewmembers were dead, Lytton's next operation was to release the Prisoner. Leaving three Troopers to secure the airlock, the others moved off at a fast jog.

CHAPTER SIX

Elsewhere on the *Vipod Mor*, with the helmet lights of Seaton and Osborn almost exhausted, the atmosphere was eerie and dispiriting. Neither was it improved by the slow progress they made as they stumbled through the liquorish-black darkness of the corridor. Ready for action, they turned into the corridor where the Prisoner's compound was located. As they approached, they saw the outer door stood open. Ancient systems malfunctioning once more – or had the compound been breached?

After checking for intruders, they cautiously entered the holding area beyond the Prisoner's cell. Directly ahead was a metre-high pedestal. Mounted on top was a lock, just a simple lock.

Osborn inserted the electronic key, but it wouldn't work. Had the thing been scratched? Why was something so vital so damned fragile? Now desperate for success, Seaton ferreted around in his trouser pocket and took out a screwdriver. He then removed the electronic key from its slot, rummaged around inside until there was a loud *click!* The rusted escutcheon plate was freed. Once the electronic key was back in place, this time the Prisoner's cell door slowly started to rise.

The area beyond was bleak and miserable. Apart from a scanner screen, a console and an ancient-looking life-support system, the walls were ugly, bare and grimy. In the middle of the area was a long transparent container in which the Prisoner, bolted to an upright frame, was sealed.

For ninety years he had been held in confinement.

Unwashed,

unseen,

unvisited

and

certainly

unloved.

Neither did it help the wellbeing of the Prisoner that, by now, almost everyone he had known would doubtless be dead.

Osborn stared into the container. Full of iced mist, it remained impossible to see anything inside.

'What if there isn't anyone in there,' she said.

Seaton quickly solved the problem by ramming his screwdriver into the drain plug and releasing the contents. Instead of returning the tool to his pocket, he offered it to Osborn. 'It's yours,' he said.

Osborn, who had recognised the screwdriver, accepted it. 'Why did you need to steal my tools?'

'To sabotage Airlock Three. The Daleks want the Prisoner.'

'But why involve you?'

Seaton shrugged. 'I s'pose they checked me out. Saw my position in the Facility.' Seaton had started to perspire, which was very unusual for him. 'I mean, two PhDs yet no proper prospects of advancement. They assumed me to be a seething mess of resentment.'

Osborn was annoyed. 'You didn't have to work for them,' she said. 'You could have moved on rather than killing your friends and fellow crewmembers.'

Seaton shook his head. 'Daleks pay very well. They even offered me eternal life. You know, make me a Dalek.'

Osborn scowled. 'Cold and brutal – that sounds just like you.'

'That's a bit harsh.' Seaton pressed the button on his laser that turned it from 'stun' to 'kill'. 'I mean, I am actually sorry about this. I was really beginning to like you.'

Suddenly a beam of white light leapt the space between Osborn and Seaton's weapon. A moment later, the girl with a beautiful smile and impressive skill at chess fell to the floor, dead.

As Seaton holstered his laser, an old-fashioned bullet was fired into the compound hitting him smack in the chest. He was dead before he hit the floor.

Lytton, with two of his Elite Guard in support, cautiously entered the compound. In his hand Lytton held a Browning

9mm automatic, an ancient Earth weapon but one he much preferred. First checking the crewmembers were both dead, the three soldiers moved to the container holding Davros, Creator of the Daleks, who appeared remarkably intact. His lower half, liveried much as a Dalek, was not only his transport but his life-support system. On his top half, with its missing left arm, Davros was dressed in the inevitable leather jacket. With blind eyes he observed the world through a single, blue electronic eyeball set into his forehead.

'Disconnect the destruct mechanism,' Lytton ordered. 'Then release Davros from this cell.'

In the cellar at Butler's Wharf, Professor Laird helped Tegan into bed and then covered her with an army blanket. Since arriving, the soldiers had unpacked additional tools that were now scattered around the floor. At one end of the table a small, makeshift laboratory had been set up. 'Sorry about the mess,' said Laird. 'We weren't expecting visitors.'

Calder, who had earlier been unable to contact the ambulance service, had again started to work on the radio. At the Doctor's suggestion, Stien had been given the remains of the sandwiches that he gratefully devoured.

With Tegan settled, Laird crossed to a large plastic bag, removed another blanket and gave it to Archer. 'For your man upstairs.' Taking the blanket, Archer nodded his thanks.

Bending down by the cylinders, the Doctor carefully inspected one. 'Have you tried to open one?'

Laird nodded. 'Didn't even scratch the casing.'

The Time Lord took out his HB pencil and, much like a child, gave one of them a gentle poke.

'Don't do that,' said Laird nervously. 'The contents could be unstable.'

Smiling, the Doctor got to his feet. 'I don't think you need worry too much.'

Archer, who was about to take the blanket upstairs, paused mid-step. 'What makes you think the cylinders are safe?'

'Don't ask me to explain at the moment, but I'm certain I've seen this sort of thing before.'

Finding the blanket uncomfortable to carry, Archer threw it over his shoulder. 'Do you think the Daleks have anything to do with this?'

The Time Lord smiled furtively. 'Knowing them as I do, it would be an enormous coincidence if they didn't.'

On that cheerless note, the Colonel left the cellar and slowly climbed the stairs to the first level of the warehouse. Lying on the floor, his body twisted at a slightly awkward angle, was the dead soldier. Unfolding the blanket, Archer spread it carefully around the soldier's body. Although he hadn't known him as a soldier, he felt the necessity to show some respect. After all, he had died defending his comrades. He was also the first man to die under Archer's command, which had unnerved him more than he expected.

With the blanket arranged as neatly as possible, Colonel Archer came to attention and, with a stiff, flat hand, saluted his dead colleague. With his duty done, he quickly returned to the cellar. 'I want you on guard upstairs,' he said to the remaining soldier.

The Doctor looked confused. 'Surely that isn't necessary. After all, this man is injured.'

'We need the area under guard. There are the remains of an alien up there, something of great scientific importance. There is also a soldier killed in the Queen's service. I wouldn't be doing my duty if I didn't show respect.'

Up on the storage level, a Dalek silently rolled out of the darkness in search of the remains of its dead colleague. Hearing voices on the floor below, it muttered quietly, but menacingly … '*Exterminate*.' Realising it could be discovered, the Dalek then entered the time corridor and was gone.

Without doubt, the Battle for the *Vipod Mor* was over. Now the Battle of the Daleks was about to begin.

In the prison compound where he had been held, Davros practised operating his life-support chariot. Ninety years of non-use had taken its toll on several key components.

Clunk! was the prominent sound when the chariot was operated. A major service was certainly needed. Unable to repair the machinery himself, Davros had demanded the services of a mechanical engineer. Instead some sort of mercenary armed to the teeth had arrived, and it soon became apparent that repairing machines was not his forte.

'Who are you?' demanded Davros.

'Commander Lytton.' The mercenary's voice was firm and with authority.

From the sea of corrugation that was Davros's face, he managed a scowl of contempt. 'Commander?' he bleeped. There followed the sound not unlike saliva being rolled into a spit bubble. 'My Daleks do not need troops.'

'No?' Lytton nodded knowingly. 'You would still be a prisoner if it weren't for my men.'

Davros smiled cheerlessly. It was his first argument in ninety years and he intended to enjoy it. 'You speak as though my Daleks are no longer capable of war.'

'A lot happened during your time in prison.'

Davros scowled again. 'I assume the conflict with the Movellans is over?'

Lytton nodded again. 'Although casualties were very high.'

Davros chortled a little louder than was prudent. 'When my Daleks are engaged, high casualties are to be expected.'

'I'm talking about *Dalek casualties.*'

Like a man with a sudden intense bout of malaria, Davros' single hand started to quiver.

'They *lost,* Davros.' Lytton's comment drove home like the winning dagger in a knife fight. 'They were totally defeated.'

Davros let out a loud, guttural grunt as he collapsed into an uncontrollable triple fit of anger, fury and confusion. His first argument in ninety years had not concluded as he would have wished.

*

Neither were things going well for Turlough.

He was lost.

Not properly lost, as he would say.

Just a bit lost. More like misdirected.

It certainly hadn't helped that patrols of Troopers kept passing by at the wrong time, forcing him to hide, leaving him disorientated. Neither was it useful that Turlough had forgotten the compass given to him by the Doctor. Then there were the wretched Daleks gliding around like so many demented pepper pots. It was like having all the school bullies crammed into one class.

Arriving at yet another door, Turlough turned the handle – nothing. All he needed was somewhere to hide, to rest before he got himself captured or killed. Headspace that might help him find the time corridor so that he could make the journey back to Earth.

Turlough tried another door. This time it silently slid open and he cautiously entered.

Brightly lit, the room was much larger than expected. In its centre were two adjacent couches covered in a pristine, white plasticised cloth. At end of each couch was a control box with an array of wires and sensors attached. Along one side of the wall were huge glass cabinets, each big enough to hold a large, prone man. The cabinets had sliding doors, the interiors of which were covered in frost.

Moving around the room, Turlough examined the other pieces of equipment, trying, unsuccessfully, to work out their use. Eventually, exhausted by the activities of the day and, in an act of utter foolishness, Turlough climbed onto one of the couches and closed his eyes. As he tried to sleep, he became aware of a faint clicking sound. Opening his eyes he noticed a badly adjusted security camera panning across the room. *Oh no,* he thought, *whoever they are, they know I'm here.* Quickly, Turlough climbed off the couch and moved towards the door. As he did, two Daleks watched via the security system.

'He is the Doctor's companion,' rasped the Alpha Dalek in full, hateful rant. 'He should be exterminated.'

The Supreme Dalek wasn't so certain. 'He would be better used as bait,' it oozed. 'The Doctor is sentimental. He will pursue the boy here. This will serve the Daleks' plan.'

The Alpha Dalek wasn't so certain. To exterminate was what it had been conditioned to do, but now it was being asked to passively ... *wait.*

That didn't correlate at all, but the Supreme Dalek wasn't prepared to concede. 'Let the boy roam,' it continued. 'Observe what he does.'

'I obey,' said the Alpha Dalek sternly ... but, in reality, it wasn't overly keen to obey anyone or anything, especially when ordered by something as effete as the Supreme Dalek.

Turlough emerged into the corridor and turned to run back towards the time corridor. As he did, a Dalek entered at the far end and started to move towards him. Turlough quickly retraced his steps taking him away from his potential escape back to Earth.

Breaking into a run, he passed from the battlecruiser into the *Vipod Mor*.

Turlough was now truly lost.

In the warehouse basement, an exhausted Stien, propped up in a chair, was sound asleep.

Sergeant Calder was on the radio. 'Zero-three to HQ. Zero-three to HQ. Over,' he called. 'Nothing, sir. There's no signal.'

'Time turbulence is masking it,' said the Doctor. 'It would be faster to telephone.'

Laird, who was adjusting Tegan's makeshift pillow, said: 'There's a phone box outside. I'll go, Colonel. You're needed here.'

Archer was far from certain. 'This is more than a military matter,' he said. 'I'll need to speak to the Ministry of Defence.'

The Doctor removed his Panama from an inside pocket, unfurled it and then placed it jauntily on his head. 'I'll come with you. I need the exercise.'

Archer shook his head. 'You're the only one who knows anything about fighting Daleks,' he cautioned, unbuckling his gun belt. 'Your duty is here.'

Reluctantly, the Doctor took the weapon. Guns weren't his style at all. Simply being near one made him ill at ease. It also reminded him how aggressive Tellurians could be. Too small for hunting, the handgun had been designed for no other purpose than killing people. This made him feel very uncomfortable.

While the Doctor looked for a safe place to store the weapon, the Colonel set out to find a telephone box. Stien started to snore in a loud, uncontrolled manner. In a way the Doctor was impressed. Stien contributed very little to the group, but somehow managed to dominate the situation, even if it were only by snoring.

On the first floor of the warehouse, a lighter sparked and puffs of smoke drifted across the storage area. Lance Corporal Miller, who was guarding the Dalek and dead soldier, puffed heavily on his cigarette. He was bored. Neither did it help that the temperature in the warehouse had dropped and that he was also feeling very cold. In an attempt to warm himself the soldier started to stamp his feet as he walked up and down. This was fine until he passed close to where the Dalek's damaged casing was stacked and heard a slithering noise.

Quickly, Miller dropped his cigarette and stepped on it. He then raised his rifle into the firing position scared of what might happen next.

In the warehouse cellar, Tegan was complaining of a terrible headache. Having acquired two paracetamol from Professor Laird, the Doctor was now feeding them to Tegan one at a time.

'I need to get out of here,' the Doctor said. 'Get back to the TARDIS.'

Sergeant Calder, who was pondering whether he should make more tea, couldn't but help hear the Doctor's remark. 'You want to go *where*, sir?'

'I need to get to my vessel and then find Turlough.'

Feeling uncomfortable, the Sergeant shuffled his feet. 'I understand how you feel, sir, but I must ask you to wait until the Colonel returns.'

The Doctor shook his head. 'I can't. Turlough could be in severe danger.'

Calder was trying his best to be sympathetic. 'I'm sure the Colonel won't be long, sir.'

But before the Doctor was able to answer, a terrible scream was hurled from the first floor. This impacted on Stien who sat bolt upright and then, to further celebrate his abrupt awakening, promptly fell off his chair. While this was happening Calder, more sensibly, had picked up the spare rifle while the Doctor snatched Archer's sidearm. With Stien grabbing a hammer from the floor for protection, the three men rushed from the cellar, taking the stairs at a phenomenal speed. Entering the first-floor storage area, they encountered the lance corporal again rolling around the floor and tearing at something on his neck. As Calder moved to the writhing soldier, the object suddenly detached itself, skittered across the floor and disappeared into a large pile of rubbish.

While Calder attended to his colleague, the Doctor picked up the stick he had played with earlier, quickly ran to the pile of sweepings and started to beat it very hard ... but the creature had gone.

'Are you all right, lad?' asked Sergeant Calder.

The soldier groaned.

'Be careful,' said the Doctor. 'Your man could be infected from the bite.'

'I was t-t-terrified,' Stien chipped in. 'I thought it was a Dalek.'

'It was,' said the Time Lord, examining the marks on the soldier's neck. 'Or at least what remains of one.'

Calder looked anxious. 'So, what do we do now?'

The Doctor was very serious. 'We find it,' he said, 'before it tries to kill again.'

Having equipped themselves with sticks, Calder, Stien and the Doctor moved around the room, rummaging in anything that could protect the remains of the Dalek. For added protection Stien carried the injured soldier's rifle, while the man himself slumped on a nearby box staring at nothing in particular.

Systematically, the group searched the area. Even though what they were looking for was unusual, the trio was surprised they hadn't found it sooner. Neither, to compensate for their disappointment, was there any sign of the entrance to the time corridor.

The men continued to search until almost every square centimetre had been inspected, that was except for two piles of dirty sacks. Cautiously, Calder approached one of the piles. As he did, one of the sacks started to move.

Not much.

Just a little.

Calder continued to search.

A minute later it moved again. This time Stien, who was searching nearby, saw it. With several jerks of his thumb, he indicated the moving sack and the Doctor silently crossed to it.

Carefully he inserted the end of his stick under the edge of the sack as Calder raised his rifle into the firing position. Poised, and ready for action, the Doctor deftly flicked away the sack…

But instead of a damaged Dalek there was a very disgruntled moggy.

Calder laughed. 'So much for the conqueror of the universe,' he chortled.

The others smiled, but it proved too soon as another terrible scream burst from the soldier. Again, he was spreadeagled across the floor, the frothing green obscenity tearing yet again at his throat. Quickly, the Doctor grabbed a sack, dropped it over the Dalek mutant and ripped it free from the soldier's neck. The creature quivered and shook, and the Doctor smashed it against the filthy floor. While it lay stunned, he tugged the sidearm from his waistband, pressed the gun's muzzle hard against the sacking and squeezed the trigger several times.

The gunshots echoed around the warehouse, booming, thumping and screaming as they went. The noise was horrible

'Is it dead?' asked Stien.

'Would you care to look?' The Doctor's reply was sharper than intended. Even though he knew that the Dalek, given half a chance, would have despatched all of them, the Time Lord nevertheless felt uncomfortable that he had killed it.

And with a hand gun!

Not wanting to hold the weapon, the Doctor slipped the gun into his pocket as the clatter of boots echoed around the storage area. Breathless, Laird rushed up the stairs. 'What happened?' she asked. 'I heard shooting.'

'The Dalek wasn't quite dead.'

As Laird and Calder prepared to take the lance corporal down to the cellar, the Doctor said to Calder, 'I know you asked me not to go, but I need to find Turlough. You should be safe from the Daleks for the time being.'

Calder frowned. 'I don't think the Colonel would like you going.'

'Then ask him to forgive me,' said the Doctor taking out Archer's gun and handing it to him. 'And please tell Tegan I'll be back for her very soon.'

As they continued towards the stairs, the Doctor turned to Stien. 'I need your help to find my companion ... and also the Dalek ship.'

Stien's face collapsed. '*Me?*' he said. 'G-g-go to the *Dalek* ship? They'll kill me.'

'But I can't do this without your help.'

'*Help?*' Stien blustered. 'You don't know how much of a coward I am.'

As Davros coughed, heaved and spluttered, Lytton watched the Creator of the Daleks physically age in front of him. It seemed even he couldn't cope with the rigours of ninety years in solitary confinement.

'Are you all right?' Lytton didn't sound entirely interested.

'There are malfunctions in my life-support system,' whined Davros. 'I need an engineer.' And as though to emphasise the fact, he let out a long, asthmatic cough followed by a toe-numbing bout of wheezing.

'You must board the Dalek ship,' insisted Lytton. 'We have everything you require.'

But Davros wasn't interested. 'In case I need stabilising I must remain close to my cryo chamber.'

Lytton explained there was a time factor, that the *Vipod Mor* had transmitted a distress signal and, with possible patrol ships in the area, a taskforce could soon be with them. The mercenary shifted uneasily. 'Will you be able to find an antidote?'

Davros nodded.

'A lot of work has already been done,' added Lytton.

The Creator wasn't impressed. 'I am Davros. The Daleks are my creation. I shall genetically re-engineer them.'

Lytton smiled. 'We have a laboratory prepared for you.'

Davros still wasn't interested. 'I shall work here. In what was my prison.'

Colonel Archer's search for a phone box was not going well. It felt as though he had been walking for hours, but in fact it was only twenty minutes. Finally finding one, he was disappointed to see the wire from the receiver hanging limply, no longer connected to the handset. His mood lifted when two police officers, complete with radio transmitters, arrived. However, the only thing they wanted to share was the view down the muzzles of two 9mm specials. These were not nice policemen, who would help you across the road, but, as Colonel Archer was about to find out, very nasty, highly motivated sociopaths.

Sent by the Supreme Dalek, Trooper Engineer Dente Kiston reported to Davros for duty. His task was to repair several non-functioning components in the Prisoner's chair. Finding Kiston a competent engineer, Davros decided to 'recruit' him. So, surreptitiously, he removed a device from a hidden compartment in his life-support system and emptied its contents into the engineer's shoulder. The mind-altering formula went to work instantly, and Kiston was enslaved to Davros.

On the bridge of the battlecruiser, the Supreme Dalek watched on a screen as Davros conditioned the engineer. 'Davros betrays the Dalek cause,' said the Alpha Dalek.

Although greatly displeased by his behaviour, the Supreme Dalek had no choice but to accept the circumstances for the time being. They needed Davros to complete all necessary research and, in the meantime he must be made to believe that they served him.

As the Alpha Dalek howled and growled largely inside its own mind regarding this decision, it received the transmission that a company of Daleks were now on their way to Earth and that the soldiers in the warehouse would be conditioned. The additional protection was ordered as precaution against further destruction of Daleks. 'The soldiers will protect the entrance to the time corridor on Earth,' ranted the Alpha Dalek. 'They will also protect the cylinders.'

The Supreme Dalek was beginning to purr. 'And what of the Doctor?'

'He will soon be on board his TARDIS with the Tellurian. They will be brought to the battlecruiser.'

If Daleks could smile, this might have been the occasion to do so. But they couldn't. So they didn't.

Lytton would have liked to have smiled too but, being in the company of Davros, it was highly unlikely to happen.

He didn't like Davros. It wasn't because the wizened creature was hateful and vicious – although clearly that didn't help – but he talked too much. Endless spiel about himself. A deadbeat's dilemma. Although on this occasion he did have some reason to complain.

'That was the place of my incarceration,' Davros snarled pointing at the glass container.

Lytton tut-tutted in sympathy.

'For ninety years I was detained in that. Ninety years of mind-destroying boredom. I was conscious during every second.'

Davros gave an involuntary yelp as Kiston's electronic probe touched something sensitive.

'The Tellurians have no stomach for judicial murder,' Davros droned. 'They prefer to leave you to slowly rot and die.' He then found his irony button. 'They call it being *humane*.'

In an attempt to ingratiate himself with Davros, Lytton said: 'Then you must be equally humane in your revenge.'

'I shall destroy Earth at my leisure,' Davros gloated. 'But first I must deal with a meddling Time Lord.'

'That has been anticipated,' Lytton was pleased to announce. 'The Doctor's capture is imminent.'

For Davros, the news was indeed good. 'Once I have drained his mind of all knowledge and information, he shall then die slowly and painfully.'

Then, like Florence Foster Jenkins aiming for a high C, he squawked: '*The Doctor has interfered for the last time!*'

Turlough was finding it more and more difficult to move around the *Vipod Mor*. Groups of Troopers patrolled almost everywhere. He feared it was only a matter of time before he was seen and a single shot from a laser rifle terminated his life.

Overwhelmed by the sensation of self-pity, Turlough continued to search for a safe place to hide. As he rounded the corner of one of the endless corridors, he almost fell over a Trooper who was bent down fastening his combat boot. Much to Turlough's amazement, he struck out with his fist and caught the Trooper hard on what was obviously a glass jaw. As the soldier hit the ground, Turlough took off at a speed he never thought possible. Back along the corridor, around more corners …

And – as luck would have it – straight into the unfriendly arms of Mercer. A second later, watched by Styles and attendant crewmembers, Turlough had been flipped onto his back.

Mercer's limited training in martial arts was nonetheless proving useful.

CHAPTER SEVEN

There it was, blue and bold, with rivulets of rain cascading down its sides.

Almost everyone who had seen the TARDIS was confused. Stien was no exception. Following the Doctor into the police box, he found everything bright, tranquil and rather large. The look on Stien's face said it all.

Bewilderment.

Amazement.

Wonderment.

'That's right,' said the Time Lord, 'it's bigger on the inside than it is on the outside.'

'I'm going mad,' groaned Stien. 'Daleks. Time corridors. Now this,' he said, indicating the console room.

The Doctor reassured him that normality would soon return, but Stien wasn't so certain. 'You s-s-say that, but will I still be sane enough to know when it happens?'

Little did he know that he had entered a physiological miracle. So, if his mind was overloaded already, wait until he saw what was beyond the console room.

There was a cornucopia of delights from the simplest to the unimaginable. The interior was a celebration of what the Doctor had seen and experienced over a very long lifetime. It had grown and metamorphosed with each regeneration, reflecting the Doctor's various selves.

The TARDIS may have been part of the Type 40 TT series from the Time Lord's planet of Gallifrey, but given the many personal modifications it had been lifted far and beyond its original specifications and design, for better or worse. It was a renegade of its type much like the Time Lord and was as quirky and unpredictable as its owner.

There was no end to its interior: it was an infinite edgeless space that allowed for all possibilities and, for that matter, improbabilities. The Doctor relished in maximising its potential, its character, its personality. So, should Stien have ventured through that console room door, he would have been astounded, overwhelmed and flabbergasted.

There were endless corridors and stairways that didn't so much lead as draw and entice you into rooms, chambers, halls, auditoriums, attics, cellars and spaces that were indefinable. These presented surprising experiences and sensations, both good and bad. This was at the heart of what the interior was about.

An art gallery was not so much an area to display paintings, sculpture or installations as a place where you would be immersed into the artwork, gaining a real understanding of the artist, their life and what fuelled their inspiration. This could be a daunting prospect given the turmoil experienced by some of the Earth artists such as Caravaggio, Rembrandt and van Gogh, but it was always revelatory and at times visceral. It was even rumoured that Michelangelo had used one of the Doctor's artist studios to paint a couple of masterpieces, but that might have been an exaggeration.

The Doctor's wardrobe was a huge cavern lined with several oceans of conflicting garments that came and went with the tides of fashion. Although the selection was massive, it was not always reflected in the Doctor's own style, which currently inclined towards the conservative.

If feeling somewhat jaded, the Explosion Emotion chamber could offer Stien the opportunity to reconnect with his past, igniting sensations simple or complex. It could be the feel of the fragile beating heart of a young puppy cradled in your arms, the smell of freshly laundered sheets or your grandfather's greenhouse bursting with moist new green growth, the taste of a good bottle of wine accompanied with exquisite cheeses and crisp crunchy celery, seeing the exhilarating colour explosion of a sunset shifting and rearranging itself to the sweet birdsong of the swift as it shot through the sky. Whether Tellurian or alien like the Doctor, your senses – whatever they were – would be awakened, tickled and surprised. The dreadful foes of the universe could have benefitted from a spell in this chamber.

If Stien needed a good read, then he could do no better than the Doctor's library. Its collection boasted books from across the cosmos from the foremost writers including philosophers, scientists, poets, dramatists and essayists. There were texts from the earliest periods of Earth – the dramas from Classical Greece, the histories of Rome (though not entirely accurate) and the science journals of nineteenth-century discoverers. The Doctor particularly liked the works of Oscar Wilde, but often confused his titles with those of William Shakespeare.

Should Stien be hungry, and he often was, he would have been spoilt for choice. The endless dishes of unsurpassed good cooking both simple and elaborate would have sated even his appetite. He would have been well advised to have the 'limited' tasting menu that at least only amounted to some 33 dishes. If he were in a hurry, then the humble but very adequate TARDIS nut roast special would have satisfied his taste buds. All the dishes were prepared by the unseen robot chef called Ooba-Doa. It was even suggested that there was a French bistro in the bowels of the TARDIS, but to the chagrin of anyone who had tried to find it, the restaurant remained elusive.

Bon appetit!

After his fine dining, Stien might have wanted to avail himself of the gym and burn off any unwanted calories. Its extensive equipment would instantly diagnose exactly the regime required and positively encourage the user to a sleeker and healthier self.

And, of course, there was always the added pleasure of endorphins. Alternatively, he could just go for a jog through the cloisters.

As he was drawn further into the time vessel, he would have noticed the eclectic Earth-design motifs adorning its corridors and rooms. For example, the Corinthian columns outside the Library, hugely elegant stone cantilevered staircases connecting one level of the TARDIS to another and of course the fine wooden hammer beam roof covering a vast banqueting hall. Elsewhere there were the firm stringent lines of the Bauhaus movement contrasting strongly with the frippery and fun of Art Deco. These were the periods of art and design the Doctor favoured. Oddly, closest to his two hearts was the work of Fred Coles, designer and manufacturer of exotic garden sheds.

If Stien had popped his head into the Cinema, the three Earth films on standby would have been *Chimes at Midnight,* directed by Orson Welles, *The Sea Hawk,* directed by Michael Curtiz,' and *The Third Man,* directed by Carol Reed, all firm favourites of the Doctor. But, of course there were many, many more cinematic treats. Popcorn, frankfurters and drinks too sugary for their own good were never allowed. Viewing films was a serious matter on board the TARDIS.

What would have puzzled Stien were the countless workshops of all shapes and sizes. At some stage in the TARDIS's existence, maybe before the Doctor's time, these workshops had been used in the working of metals such as gold, silver and tinclavic from the mines of Raaga, as well some of the newer alloys from the How Lee Collection of Galaxies. No one ever questioned how these metals arrived on board the TARDIS or indeed who would have used them. The mystery was that someone, somewhere, at some time, thought this was a useful idea. And if Ooba-Doa ever used them furtively when cooking, he was far too discreet to advertise the fact.

In recognition of the botanic splendour of two great gardens – Babylon and Kew – the Doctor had developed his own inventive style of cultivation. This involved extensive use of a man cave in the form of a Fred Coles shed where he potted up his favourite plant, *Apium graveolens,* on his personal and very private allotment.

No visitors allowed.

Visitors could, however, have browsed his fine collection of geological specimens. Some people collect stamps, others use metal detectors, but if you are the Doctor you collect from around the universe some 40,000 tons of mixed rocks. These contained the indisputable evidence of the Big Bang theory.

As with other spaces in the TARDIS, the Concert Room was a phenomenon and would have offered Stien whatever music suited his mood or indeed instruments he wished to play. If he wanted to broaden his repertoire, there were the romantic five, Tchaikovsky being one – who could not be touched by his *Swan Lake*? Or he could be moved by the music from the Baroque period and hear Johann Sebastian Bach's rousing *Brandenburg Concertos*. If classical music wasn't for him, then he could tap his toes away to some jazz, bop like the best of them to the enduring Rolling Stones, or gyrate to the best bands of the Second and Third Quartz.

In spite of the vastness of the TARDIS, on a more prosaic level, much of the everyday life on board took place in more manageable-sized domestic rooms. These were much cosier and intimate places.

And there was much, *much* more.

The Doctor's insatiable desire to keep so much in the TARDIS might seem insane …

… but sanity was becoming a sort of running theme. Certainly, holding someone against the wall and punching them very hard, was not the best way to maintain it. Styles looked on as Mercer interrogated Turlough further, repeatedly asking the same question about where the Daleks had concentrated their main force. Of course, Turlough didn't know, so the questioning and beating continued until Styles could tolerate it no longer.

'Stop!' she shouted. 'Even a thickhead like you must realise he doesn't know anything. Look at his clothes, he isn't a Dalek Trooper.'

Mercer stopped beating Turlough.

For once in his life, the Brendon schoolboy was grateful for wearing the uniform he had yet to jettison.

Slowly, Mercer nodded. Why hadn't he noticed the uniform himself? He decided he was losing it in a big way. The thought of destroying the *Vipod Mor* had thrown him off balance. In the space of what felt like a few minutes, he had slipped from potential captain to a fugitive aboard his own spacecraft.

This, he decided, was not the best career move he could have made.

Styles was also trying to hold it together. Although she didn't look forward to dying, she was aware there was no other choice. This was the necessary price in order to eradicate Davros. To deliberately kill was a hideous thing for a medical doctor to undertake, but the prospect of allowing Davros to arbitrarily destroy countless children was still more abhorrent.

Meanwhile, in the warehouse, the lance corporal was in a different sort of pain.

Calder, agreeing with Tegan that Colonel Archer had been gone too long, left to search for him. For reasons unknown, the sergeant's departure seemed to upset the injured lance corporal. At first, he developed breathing problems and, when he tried to stand, he wobbled so badly he fell over. Regaining his balance, he started to walk around the cellar. Pausing by the makeshift laboratory, he began to rummage in the glass containers on the table.

'That's dangerous,' Laird shouted. 'There's acid in some of the bottles.'

'*And there's also a gun on the table,*' said Tegan, urgently pointing.

'Looks like the Colonel's,' Laird said looking at it closely.

Hearing this seemed to send the lance corporal off into another turmoil.

As Tegan pulled herself upright in bed, she said to the solider, 'Come on. You're excused duties. Relax.'

But Lance Corporal Miller wasn't interested. Before Laird could pick up the gun, he let out another shocking scream, pushed her to one side and knocked over the table. Compelled by the Dalek infection in his bloodstream, he then fled from the warehouse, along Shad Thames and stopped by a three-ton lorry newly parked at the side of the road. Seated in the cab were two familiar policemen. Without hesitating, he threw open the back doors and climbed inside. Spread across the floor of the lorry, in between containers of electronic equipment, were the corpses of his colleagues.

It would have taken another Time Lord even more experienced than the Doctor to adequately explain the process that was about to take place inside the lorry. Equally it would have taken someone of similar capabilities to explain what was happening in the warehouse in Shad Thames.

A rudimentary description would be to call it time travel. A more sophisticated explanation would require a double-first in mathematics plus the help of a dozen Albert Einsteins and several Stephen Hawkings on the side just to interpret the first five lines of the principle.

Inside the warehouse, it was very dark.

Outside, rain continued to pour.

And it was getting colder.

On the first floor of the warehouse, the atmosphere was now ghostly, as if a vampire had caressed the soul of a saint.

Between the two tea chests that marked the entrance to the time corridor, four Daleks started to develop, spinning like a runaway whirlpool as they appeared to emerge through the floor.

'The Supreme Dalek orders the duplication of the soldiers,' trumpeted the group leader on arrival. 'They will be released to take control of the warehouse.'

'We obey,' echoed the reply.

A receiver inside the second Dalek's dome clicked on and the duplication signal begun to be transmitted with a terrible *weeeeening* sound.

In the cellar below, the nerve-splitting sound sliced into the room, forcing Laird and Tegan to clamp their hands over their ears.

'What's happening?' shouted Laird.

'How do I know? I'm from Australia.'

Laird tried to laugh, but her sense of despair would only allow the tiniest of tiny smiles to unfurl.

On the upper floor of the warehouse, the group leader confirmed they must now return to the Supreme Dalek's base as the duplication of the soldiers had been successful. The transmission field was then reversed and the Daleks re-entered the time corridor and disappeared.

In Shad Thames, the doors of the white three-ton lorry opened and, to all intents and purposes, out stepped Colonel Archer, Sergeant Calder and two soldiers. Their uniforms were pristine and they were all fully armed. The squad came to attention, saluted and set off towards the warehouse at a fast march.

*

With the high-pitched *weeeeening* sound gone, Tegan and Laird removed their hands from their ears. The relief was tangible.

'What caused that?' said Tegan.

The professor shook her head.

'This is getting weird,' Tegan reflected. 'Even weirder than before, and that was weird enough.'

Just then the canvass curtain was pulled back with a mighty *SWISH!* Standing in the gap were Colonel Archer and his squad.

Tegan and Laird were delighted by their return.

'What went wrong?' asked the professor. 'What was that dreadful sound?'

But instead of a friendly response, the soldiers were stony-faced.

'There's nothing to worry about,' said Archer almost angrily. 'I'm fully in control of the situation.'

Which was much as Davros felt.

Lytton switched off his helmet radio. 'Your laboratory is ready. It's here on the *Vipod Mor,* close to your cryo chamber.'

Davros nodded. 'In addition to Kiston, I also need the assistance of a chemist.'

'It will be provided.'

No sooner had Lytton agreed, then the door to the prison compound slid open to reveal two waiting Daleks.

'Guards?' Davros enquired quizzically.

'A simple precaution, Davros. There are members of the station's crew still at large.'

'You should know,' Davros gave a small croaky laugh, 'that I am very difficult to kill.'

Flanked by his evil creations, Davros led the way along the corridor. Kiston followed a few paces behind.

In many respects this was already a procession of war in the making.

Tegan and Laird had been watching the unusual behaviour of Colonel Archer. For some reason, he had ordered his men to the upper floor where the entrance to the time corridor was hidden. From what little they had gleaned, the Colonel had ordered the rest of his squad not to talk to them.

Tegan was further concerned by the sudden crisp freshness of their attire, as though they had changed into new uniforms. It was then she noticed that Archer was wearing the sidearm he had loaned the Doctor, in fact the same one that was now lying on the floor by the makeshift lab. For that to have happened, the Colonel's gun had to have been somehow duplicated …

'I don't think that's Colonel Archer,' Tegan whispered.

'Then who can it be?'

Both women were now feeling very uncomfortable. Even an innocent enquiry about the ambulance was curtly dismissed.

'This warehouse is now under martial law,' Archer announced, glaring at Tegan and Laird. 'If you attempt to leave, you will be shot.'

*

In the TARDIS, things felt just as dangerous. The Doctor was moving around the console, flicking switches, turning knobs and doing all sorts of other complex things. At last he managed to locate the Dalek ship on the deep-space scanner. This was obviously not what Stien had wanted to hear.

Seeing his worried expression, the Doctor said: 'If you are really that worried, I could take you back to the warehouse. But if you do decide to stay, you will be perfectly safe in the TARDIS.'

Stien, mustering up his last three scoops of bravery, confirmed he would go with him.

Smiling, the Doctor operated more switches on the console and activated the time rotor. The TARDIS went through its usual start-up symphony of grunts and assorted noises. Everything seemed to be going well until there was a sudden scream from the engine and the axis of the floor turned forty-five degrees. Hanging on to the console, Stien asked desperately. 'What's h-h-happening?'

The Doctor, examining his instrumentation again, was horrified to see that the TARDIS had been dragged into the Dalek's time corridor. At least, he thought, on this occasion, it would be a quick and direct journey.

He also anticipated the welcome, on his arrival, from a gloating Supreme Dalek, keen to boast of obscene experimentation and plans for yet more horrific wars.

Hey, ho – never a quiet day!

*

Judiciously hidden around the reception area of the battlecruiser, a dozen of Lytton's Elite Guard were ready for the Doctor's arrival. Lytton, mindful of the Supreme Dalek's threat, had prepared for every contingency. Even a mouse wearing a heavily greased overcoat could not slip in or out of the area. No cheese, today.

The Doctor was suspicious when, in spite of the TARDIS having been yanked along the Dalek's time corridor, their arrival on the battlecruiser was surprisingly without incident.

'Trap or not, I need to find Turlough,' he announced.

Switching on the scanner screen, he saw the reception area was empty. He cautiously opened the door, peered out of the TARDIS and, surprisingly followed by a fully composed Stien, entered the reception area.

After looking around for a moment, the Doctor called Turlough's name.

No response.

Stealthily he moved to the entrance of the corridor.

He called again.

This time, there was a response, not from his companion, but from a member of Lytton's Elite Guard. With his weapon raised, the soldier moved towards the Doctor. The Time Lord reacted quickly, grabbing the barrel of the weapon, twisting it to break the attacker's grip and sending the Trooper tumbling over an outstretched leg.

The Doctor saw Stien removing a weapon from a rack of machine pistols. 'Quickly,' he urged him. 'Back into the TARDIS.'

Stien didn't move. Instead he pointed the gun at the Time Lord.

'This is madness!' said the Doctor. 'The Daleks won't thank you for capturing me, they'll kill you.'

Stien moved towards him. 'I didn't quite tell you the truth,' he said. 'I *serve* the Daleks. I'm a Dalek agent.'

No sooner had he said this, than Daleks and Troopers poured into the area and advanced towards a distraught Doctor.

Lytton strode in and joined Stien to watch as a Dalek pressed the Doctor hard against the wall. 'I am the Alpha Dalek.'

Alpha Dalek! That's a new title, thought the Doctor.

'You will obey me,' it continued to rasp. 'You will bend to the power of the Dalek race.'

Inside his head, the Time Lord smiled. The title might be new, but the rhetoric was just as jaded.

'You will follow me, Doctor. If you try to escape you will be *exterminated!*'

Although the Doctor had been threatened by the Daleks many times before, his rude health attested to their wanton lack of success. Unfortunately, the tone of this Dalek suggested it might be the one to succeed.

'You will not resist. You will be taken to the Duplication Chamber,' the Alpha Dalek snorted as it prodded the Doctor across the reception area.

Lytton and Stien continued to watch as the Time Lord entered an adjacent corridor and was gone.

'Impulsive, aren't they?' said Stien eventually.

Lytton, who was trying to appear cool, examined the fingernails on his right hand. 'They'd kill anyone, even if they needed them.'

Stien slotted his machine pistol into its security rack. 'Which raises an obvious question, dear boy. How long before they come for us?'

Even in the few minutes since returning to the battlecruiser, Stien had changed. His stammer had gone. He was far more confident. He had also, apparently, developed the annoying habit of calling men 'dear boy'. It seemed as if Stien had undergone some sort of weird metamorphosis.

Although Turlough was uncertain what Mercer and Styles were about, his easy charm had gained him a degree of acceptance. It always surprised him that when under pressure, he could deliver convincing patter. He could only hope that he would continue to persuade Mercer and Styles of his usefulness.

Keeping close, almost in too tight a formation, Turlough, Styles and three crewmembers moved stealthily along the corridor. Mercer, who was covering the rear, stumbled and almost toppled into a narrow spur in the corridor. 'I think it's here,' he called.

As the rest of the group retraced their steps, Mercer checked the area for guards.

Much as at a birthday party, when wildly anticipated presents are about to be opened, a frisson of excitement spread throughout the group.

Turlough was confused. 'What's the elation about?'

'We've found the Self-Destruct Chamber,' said Styles with a grin.

'But why so excited?'

Styles started to laugh like a demented thing. 'It's fun time. Now we get to blow ourselves up!'

In the basement of the warehouse, things were extra tense.

'Would anyone like tea?' asked Laird. There was no response from Archer.

'Well, as we don't know when the ambulance will arrive, then yes please,' said Tegan.

'You will receive attention as soon as it is available,' Archer bleated like an automaton.

'Thanks very much!' muttered an annoyed Tegan.

Archer was about to leave the room when he noticed the gun that the lance corporal had knocked to the floor and picked it up.

Tegan and Laird swapped glances as he left the area. They now knew that he knew that they knew that there were two identical guns.

'Pity he didn't want any tea.' Laird held up a small test tube containing a colourless liquid. 'He'd have slept for hours.'

Clambering off the bed with as much urgency as her injury allowed, Tegan walked to the trench where two of the cylinders had been freed from the compacted soil. 'Why are they so light?'

Laird shook her head. 'All my tests and attempts to open them failed.'

'We've got to get out of here somehow,' said Tegan

*

Archer climbed the stairs to the time corridor level where Calder and the two soldiers stood silently to attention. He held up the anomalous gun.

'They know we're duplicates,' said Archer. 'We must inform the Supreme Dalek.'

Under an escort of Daleks and Lytton's Troopers, the Doctor approached the Duplication Chamber. As they arrived, the door slid open. Inside it was very dark. The Time Lord could just make out several bodies lying on the floor. As his eyes adjusted to the gloom, he could just see these were the 'original' now dead bodies of Archer, Calder and the lance corporal.

'Did you have to?' said the Doctor indicating the bodies.

'Proceed! Orders must be obeyed!' insisted the Dalek. 'Compassion is forbidden! You must enter the Duplication Chamber.'

Dr Elizabeth Styles would have been furious to see Davros parked in the middle of her beautiful medical room. It had taken forever to acquire the necessary funding, an age to procure the new equipment and a ridiculous amount of time to have it installed. Styles had spent many productive hours maintaining the good health of the Facility's crew and now the medical room was being used to help the Daleks' hateful cause.

Having just inspected the area and done nothing but complain, Davros muttered, 'Primitive ... but adequate.'

The Gamma Dalek had spent the last hour fussing around, trying to be very important and mentioning the Supreme Dalek's title every five and a half seconds. Instead, what it should have been doing was to encourage the Creator of the Daleks to be more expeditious with his research.

Davros slipped on his haughtiest expression. 'I must have a sample of Movellan virus and two living Daleks for experimentation.'

The Gamma Dalek's persona exploded into a cloud of splutter and indignation. 'The use of Dalek flesh is forbidden without the express consent of the Supreme Dalek.'

'Then I suggest you acquire it at once,' Davros growled. 'Already I grow impatient.'

Meanwhile in another part of the *Vipod Mor,* Styles, Mercer and Turlough were studying the electronics that controlled the priming and detonation of the Self-Destruct device.

Dominating the room was a dome-shaped structure housing the explosives. Bathed in a ghostly blue haze, the mood of the area very much reflected the function of what was effectively the station's very own Doomsday machine.

Turlough felt that his new friends had become over-zealous with their constant dialogue about self-destruction. The thought of expiring in such a place was too depressing, especially as he was still very much attached to his current, desultory lifestyle. 'Look,' he said. 'With all this talk of blowing up the ship, is it absolutely necessary we die as well?'

Styles narrowed her eyes to the tiniest of scrutinising slits. 'You know a way out?' she snapped.

Turlough was suddenly very exuberant. 'The time corridor I mentioned. It exists. We could use it to escape.'

Uncertain, Styles hesitated.

'No harm in checking it out, then?' said Mercer, cutting in.

'Let me show you,' said Turlough.

Without another word, Turlough and Mercer left. Dodging the squads of patrolling Troopers, they made their way towards Airlock Three.

Little did they know that they had been overhead on the security system by the Supreme Dalek. Without hesitation, it ordered Lytton to isolate the Self-Destruct device and terminate the traitors.

'Nothing must endanger Davros. The hostiles must be destroyed. The Daleks must be obeyed!'

IT SEEMED THE WAR OF THE DALEKS WAS GOING VERY WELL.

CHAPTER EIGHT

Back in the Duplication Chamber, guarded by two Troopers, the Doctor sat on one of the couches and fiddled with the connecting wires to a control box.

'Do not touch the equipment,' snapped the Beta Dalek.

The Doctor raised his eyebrows. 'What will you do if I don't?'

'You will obey!'

The Doctor slipped off the end of the couch as Stien, now smartly dressed in his Trooper's uniform, came into the room. 'Without the threat of death,' the Time Lord continued. 'You have no real power.'

The Beta Dalek made a sudden move to strike, but the Doctor deftly stepped to one side and the Dalek missed.

'It is unwise to provoke them, old boy.'

The Time Lord turned in the direction of the familiar voice. 'Sergeant Stien. Love the uniform. I didn't realise you were one of Lytton's gang.'

Stien picked an almost invisible thread from his sleeve. 'He's a great soldier.'

The Doctor huffed and puffed for moment. 'The last time I met Lytton was in Soho. He was running a high-class jazz club in Old Compton Street. Apparently, it was doing very well. Even though the local murder rate trebled … but that's not unusual when Lytton's around.'

'Not only is it unwise to provoke the Daleks, the same applies to me.'

The Doctor chuckled. 'Some people are far too sensitive. Not everything I do is provocative. And, by the way, why isn't Davros here for this momentous occasion?'

'He is otherwise detained,' said Stien.

The Doctor's face lit up. 'Ah, so he is here!'

The Beta Dalek snarled, 'This does not concern you'.

'So what sort of trouble are you in this time?' mused the Doctor.

Stien was irritated. 'You must stop the questions, old boy. It causes vexation. They'll punish you.'

The Time Lord's face transmogrified into a sheen of mock amazement. 'I'm in the Duplication Chamber. Can it really get any worse?'

'Oh yes,' said Stien. 'They can make your death much more painful and undignified.'

But the Time Lord wasn't convinced. 'Not yet,' he paused. 'Not if you plan to duplicate me.' The Doctor pointed at the console at the top of the couch. 'You'll need my brain intact for that thing.'

In the warehouse, Tegan and Laird had placed one of the cylinders under the blanket on the bed to give the impression of someone asleep. This they hoped would create a diversion so they could escape. Unfortunately, their handiwork wasn't very convincing, but the sound of approaching footsteps outside certainly was. Quickly, Tegan got back into bed and pulled the blanket tightly around her and the cylinder.

Swish! The tarpaulin was pulled back and Colonel Archer entered the area.

'You can stop pretending you don't know what's happening. You are to be transferred to the Dalek ship.'

'Tegan is sick. She's very ill.'

Archer gave a look of utter contempt and, as he left, said menacingly, 'Not for much longer.'

His words only served to convince them that they needed to do something very quickly to get away.

Pulling another cylinder into the bed, they rearranged the blanket for better effect. But the harder they teased the covering, the less convincing it became.

'That isn't going to deceive anyone,' said Laird. 'Not unless there's someone here to help it along with a little bluff.' Laird gently steered Tegan towards the tarpaulin. 'Go! Find help.'

'I can't leave you—'

'You don't have a choice. Please, Tegan. The sooner you go, the sooner you'll be back with people who can make a difference.'

Reluctantly Tegan left. Slowly she made her way along the shadowy walls until she arrived at a door. Finding it had been locked, probably by Colonel Archer, she moved further on in search of another way out.

Standing on guard at the top of the corridor containing the Self-Destruct Chamber, one of the *Vipod Mor* crewmembers, weapon in hand, stood on guard. Expecting trouble, the guard was very tense and extra vigilant.

But this didn't save him.

There was a sudden swish of a blade and the guard's life was over.

Lytton and his Troopers had arrived.

In the Self-Destruct Chamber, another crewmember, Zena, studied the closed-circuit monitor covering the outside corridors. If she had been truly observant, she would have seen the flash of a knife and caught a glimpse of the Trooper's hand wielding it.

Styles was seated in front of a self-destruct computer, attempting to find a way into the system, but all she located was:

ACCESS TO SELF-DESTRUCT PROCEDURE IS CLASSIFIED INFORMATION. INSERT YOUR SECURITY CLEARANCE NUMBER.

Without such a code they could not activate the system.

And of course, they didn't have one.

Snatching up her personal radio, she attempted to call Mercer, hoping he would have the code, but heavy static from the damaged comms system prevented her from making contact. Why had the fool gone off with the boy on this wild goose chase? She turned to Zena. 'See if you can locate Mercer's whereabouts on the security cameras.'

Fingers pirouetted across a keyboard and a sequence of corridor shots flashed up on the monitor. Suddenly, Lytton and his Troopers appeared on the screen. 'That's outside in the corridor!' said another crewmember.

'Seal the unit!' ordered Styles.

Quickly, shutters were slid into the closed position and electronic bolts locked into place.

In the corridor outside, Lytton started his counter-attack by first shooting out the security cameras. Having examined the structure of the shutters sealing the unit, he knew he couldn't afford to spend an inordinate amount of time trying to break in. He therefore ordered high explosives to be used. This was ironic, given the amount of combustible material already contained in the Self-Destruct device just on the other side of the door.

But it was one of those days.

In the Duplication Room, with his coat removed, the Doctor was prostrate on the couch with sensors snaking from his head like some electronic Medusa.

In spite of the pain, he continued to annoy the Beta Dalek with more provocative questions.

'I assume one of my duplicates is destined for experimentation by Davros? You must need his services very badly.'

The Beta Dalek slipped into full rant: 'We are the superior being. Do not ask questions.'

But the Doctor wouldn't leave it there. 'It was Stien, a living, thinking human who ensnared me, not some tin-pot machine.'

'Stien is a duplicate. He is the product of our genetic engineering,' crowed the Beta Dalek.

The Time Lord looked at Stien. 'Interesting,' he said. 'Do you ever wonder what happened to the real you?'

Airlock Three was a mess. As Mercer and Turlough arrived, Styles's message came through the static, telling them she was under siege. At that moment Mercer realised his duty was to go back and do what he could to help.

'You can't go back!' Turlough was stunned. 'We have to proceed. The time corridor is just over there.'

'And the Troopers guarding it?'

'Kill them.'

'And have Daleks crawling all over us?'

Mercer placed the muzzle of his gun against Turlough's head. 'We go back.'

Reluctantly, Turlough did as he was told. He couldn't make up his mind whether to cooperate with Mercer or simply run for it.

Mercer would probably shoot him. If he didn't, then the Troopers guarding Airlock Three certainly would. On Earth, this would be called a dilemma.

On board the *Vipod Mor*, this was just part of everyday life.

Lytton and his Troopers had worked quickly. Small areas on the outside wall of the Self-Destruct Chamber had been selected to mount explosives.

Under other circumstances, a minor skirmish like this would be of no interest to him, but his sense of honour was never satisfied when fighting civilians. The odds weren't fair and the high casualty rates reeked of murder. This made Lytton uneasy. He knew he should no longer accept commissions from the Daleks but, like so many mercenaries, he acknowledged the fees were good. Exceptionally good.

At the far end of the corridor, Mercer and Turlough furtively inched their heads around the corner and quickly observed the extent of Lytton's preparations. It didn't take long for them to decide that, with only one gun between them, to attack would be futile.

'We can't help your friends now,' Turlough insisted.

'We must try something.'

'Yes, the time corridor! To escape back to Earth, and the Doctor.' Turlough had terrible imaginings of the Doctor giving up on him, of him and Tegan going back to Brendon School with the sad news of their former pupil's valiant death in a corner of a very foreign field ...

Mercer shook his head. 'Listen, why are the Troopers trying to break into the Self-Destruct Chamber? Why don't they just take Davros and leave?'

Turlough stifled a small yawn. 'Tell me?'

'For some reason, Davros can't or won't leave the *Vipod Mor,*' said Mercer. 'This gives us an opportunity to fight back. Even kill him.'

Turlough didn't like the sound of any of this, but was stuck with his current predicament. He wasn't certain what he feared most, dying a hero or being celebrated as one by his wearisome *alma mater*.

Meanwhile, the chemist Davros had requested arrived followed by one of Lytton's Troopers. Within seconds, Kiston had done his work and they were both conditioned. Davros' plan was gaining momentum.

'My army continues to grow,' he purred.

Some progress was also being made in the Self-Destruct Chamber. Banks of electronics were now spread across the floor, and Dr Styles was trying to make sense of the system. If only she had listened more attentively during the lectures on mechanical and electronic engineering. Much in the way the Doctor maintained the TARDIS, a lot of kicking, hitting and banging had taken place, producing only limited success and unnerving the other trapped crewmembers.

Desperate to find a solution, Styles thought back to her infancy when she had first played with a computer. What was the first thing she was taught to do should the computer freeze?

Reboot!

Disengage the system!

Then re-engage.

She did so. And like the proverbial Christmas tree, the computer lit up and became active.

'We've made it!' she bawled. 'We're in!'

But no one wanted to celebrate. Zena just looked at her. 'Getting in is going to be the very last thing that happens to us,' she said, ashen faced. 'Isn't it?'

Styles half-smiled. 'If we're lucky.'

It was very sad.

In the Duplication Chamber, the Doctor was less than ecstatic as he lay spreadeagled across the couch.

The Beta Dalek began to rage. 'You procrastinate. You must not resist the mind processing.'

'Tell me,' said the Doctor. 'Have the soldiers from the warehouse been duplicated?'

'Yes,' Stien grunted. 'Low-grade surface copies.' He was preoccupied with attaching further electrodes to the Time Lord's head.

'It's very clever,' the Doctor almost mocked. 'Would you like to tell me how it's done?'

'No.'

'Then what about Tegan?' The Doctor's tone was insistent.

'She's our prisoner.'

'She's harmless! You must release her,' the Doctor demanded.

The Beta Dalek had had enough. 'Show him.'

Buttons were pressed, levers pulled and frost crackled as a huge glass door slid open allowing icy air to pour into the room. As the mist cleared, the outline of a recumbent Tegan took shape.

'*No!*' the Doctor roared. 'You can't do this.'

'This is only the husk of a duplicate,' said Stien. 'She's a mere dummy, no more than an outline drawn in the snow. She's not yet activated.'

From his position on the couch, the Doctor strained at the electrodes attached to his head to see the husk of Tegan.

'Why?' demanded the Doctor.

'The Doctor without his companions would be rather incongruous,' said Stien.

'Why are you doing this?' demanded the Doctor.

'You are to return to Gallifrey,' insisted the Beta Dalek, 'where, at our command, your duplicate will assassinate the members of the High Council.'

'*No!*'

The implication was massive. Time itself would be distorted, generating havoc. With the Time Lords dead, the Daleks would be free to take over and to continue unhindered with their plan to rule the universe.

Here we go again, thought the Doctor. 'Trying to build empires on the back of the dead never works. Kill the Time Lords and you make war on Time itself – all you will get is chaos. And where there is chaos, disaster follows. Have you not learned that?'

'The Daleks make their own history,' was the emphatic response. 'The Time Lords will die and we will control the universe.'

However, in Styles's laboratory, Davros would not have agreed. The only leader of the universe, he fancied, was himself.

While Kiston and the chemist prepared further batches of Davros's conditioning formula, the Trooper stood on guard. For the first time in ninety years, Davros was exercising his mind. It wasn't often that he felt pleased but the simple task he was engaged in satisfied him enormously. Things got even better with the arrival of the Delta and Epsilon Daleks.

'We have been sent by the Supreme Dalek,' announced Delta.

'We are to assist in your research,' added Epsilon.

'I need Dalek tissue, not help,' barked Davros.

Delta confirmed that consent had been granted for their tissue to be used. There was a loud click followed by an electronic hum as the two Daleks released their locking clamps and allowed their domes to tilt forward. Revealed inside both Daleks was the mutated tissue of the Kaled race, the creature engineered by Davros himself, long ago, into the being that powered the Daleks.

To Davros, the green, quivering morasses were a beautiful sight. 'In no way will my experiment harm you,' he said. 'In fact, you will be considerably invigorated.'

Kiston stepped forward, took out the device he had used earlier and injected both Daleks.

'Perfect. Reseal your casings,' purred the Creator of the Daleks. As the domes closed, he commanded: 'Now … who do you obey?'

'We obey Davros. He is our master,' came in reply as an almost religious chant.

Pleased with events, Davros turned to Kiston. 'Now, what is delaying my sample of the Movellan virus?'

'The virus is too dangerous to store on board the Dalek ship,' said Kiston. 'Samples are kept on Earth. The Supreme Dalek has already made arrangements for transportation.'

Tegan had finally found a ground-floor window she hoped she could open. Dragging a crate to the bottom of its frame, she clambered onto the box and struggled to release its catch.

It didn't move.

Looking around, she found a baton of wood and started to lever against the obstruction.

It still didn't budge.

Tegan searched some more and found a piece of gas cannon and was able to lever the catch open. Summoning up what was left of her strength, she slid the window open and climbed out. The ground was much further away than she expected so, positioning herself to hang from the window ledge, she lowered herself down, released her grip and fell the remaining two feet.

Bump!

Picking herself up, she stumbled off along the road not fully knowing where she was going.

Turlough and Mercer cautiously made their way along the corridor to what had been Davros's prison. It didn't take long to establish that its occupant was no longer in residence.

'We're too late,' whispered Turlough.

Mercer wasn't interested in hearing the obvious. 'He has to be nearby. He can't be that far away.'

Turlough was not in a mood to search the entire ship, not with so many Daleks and Troopers at large. 'Find him yourself.'

Mercer pushed his laser rifle against Turlough's head. 'We'll find him together.'

Turlough knew he had no choice but to continue with Mercer.

Such was life – and, more than likely, death.

Alone in the warehouse basement, Laird was startled by an electronic buzz. The noise intensified to a level of being unbearable.

Clasping her hands to her ears, she turned to see one of the alien cylinders slowly dissolve and disappear.

The Doctor, his hands and feet strapped to the couch, was having the final electrodes attached to his head.

'Stien, you must proceed alone.' said the Beta Dalek. 'I have been summoned to other duties.'

Seeing it move to the door, the Doctor called out. 'Not staying to the bitter end. How disappointing.'

'When it is time to die, you will, in your agony, beg to pay homage to the Daleks.' And with that fond farewell, it was gone.

His conversation with Stien didn't go any better.

'Why do they take themselves so seriously?' asked the Doctor.

'I warned you not to provoke the Daleks. It can only make things worse.'

'Just get on with it,' said the Doctor.

'Do you think I-I-I enjoy ...' Stien's voice trailed off. 'Do you think I have a ch-ch-choice?'

Confused by the sudden change of mood, the Doctor stared up at Stien. For a moment, he was convinced he saw a tear ... but then it was gone.

One of the cylinders, originally stored in the warehouse at Shad Thames, was carried from the entrance of the Dalek time corridor into the battlecruiser's reception area.

Supervised by the Alpha Dalek, two Troopers were instructed to take it to Davros's laboratory aboard the *Vipod Mor*.

They moved off, escorted by three additional Troopers, laser rifles at the ready.

It seemed no chances were being taken.

With groups of crewmembers still active, the escort moved cautiously out of the reception area, through the scorched remains of Airlock Three and into the *Vipod Mor*. With further Troopers lining the corridors, the escort party moved towards their destination.

Having squeezed themselves into a narrow service shaft, Turlough and Mercer watched through a crack in the casing as the escort team passed by.

'Why does such a small cylinder command so big an escort?' whispered Mercer. 'And where is it being taken?'

Turlough wasn't sure he wanted to know.

'Looks like it's heading in the direction of the Medical Facility. That's the only logical explanation.'

Turlough was becoming more uncomfortable with each word Mercer muttered.

'The content of the cylinder is vital to someone.'

Turlough began to feel sick. He now knew the D-word was about to be mentioned.

'It has to be on its way to Davros.'

That was the D-word Turlough didn't want to hear.

'Which means he must be using the Medical Facility,' concluded Mercer.

Turlough was horrified. 'We can't go there! Look at the escort. The place will be surrounded.'

Realising Turlough was right, Mercer reluctantly agreed to retrace their steps and find somewhere more suitable to hide.

CHAPTER NINE

Meanwhile, Tegan had found her way back into Shad Thames. She knew she had to find help for Laird from somewhere and wondered whether she should go to the police. Colonel Archer had done precisely that and he and his fellow soldiers had finished up as semi-zombies. Alternatively, she could try to find a pub full of hale and hearty drinkers, but that was unlikely in an area almost devoid of residents. This left her with the most obvious option. She should return to the TARDIS.

Reaching the derelict Old Custom House, with its ever so spooky atmosphere, she turned towards the river eager to get back to the time machine. Increasing her speed, she turned onto to the wharf and was horrified to find the TARDIS had gone.

Thinking it might have been moved by the Doctor, she ran over to the floodwall and saw that the tide was out. On the mud flat below, all she could see was a man wearing waders with earphones clamped to his head and metal detector in hand, scavenging the riverbed for buried treasure.

But no TARDIS.

Tegan started to walk back to Shad Thames. As she did, two policemen turned onto the wharf. *Help at last,* she thought.

Until she saw one of them carrying an automatic revolver.

Quickly, she turned back and ran along the wharf pursued by the policemen. Arriving at the steps leading down to the riverbed, she saw the metal detectorist below. Desperate for help, she called out to him, but his headphones stopped him hearing her.

Now desperate for help, Tegan started to descend the steps to the river. As she did, the policemen caught up with her. One of them levelled his gun at her but, instead of shooting Tegan, he turned it onto the man on the mudflat and fired.

To the sound of Tegan screaming, the man on the mudflats toppled over and died.

'No!' she shouted, swinging round to the policeman. His gun was now pointed at her face. He gestured that she should come with him back to the warehouse.

Tegan stared down at the body sprawled alone on the muddy sand, wondering who he'd been. A man who had been killed just because she had called out to him – a call he'd never even heard.

PJ, who was in his mid-sixties, had prospected this very area dozens of times before, his biggest and best finds being a Roman coin from the Claudian period and what people said was a quill pen from the study of Samuel Pepys.

He enjoyed the quiet time away from the busy hurly-burly of London life. Paradoxically, he felt safe down there on his patch. Today he had arrived earlier than usual, not having met up with his mate, Mr Jones, with his amazing cigarette tin, at their regular café. He would never know that his friend had died earlier in Shad Thames, killed by the same fake policemen.

Escorted by those uniformed murderers, a dejected Tegan was forced back towards the warehouse.

All hope lost.

Her soul aching…

Her heart broken.

Inside the Self-Destruct Chamber, it was very hot. Styles's hair clung to her forehead and cheeks. Progress had been slow but things were beginning to get there. She tapped a combination of switches and suddenly a loud whine came from the console. It was as though a heavy-duty electric motor had been turned on and was running up to speed.

Pleased for a moment with the breakthrough, Styles was struck with the horrible realisation once more that should she get to operate the Self-Destruct device, it would be the last thing she'd ever do.

In the corridor outside, the explosive charges were in place and two of Lytton's Elite Guard had managed to bypass one of the door's mechanisms. It was now just a matter of Lytton giving the order.

Inside the Chamber, a computer monitor chimed a warning.

'The door,' said Zena, tapping desperately at her comms handset. 'They're going to breach it.'

'We have to hold out!' Frantically, Styles worked at the controls. 'We need just a few more minutes ...'

But only moments were left to them now.

The door flew open followed by the blast of several laser rifles. Zena and the other two crewmembers were cut down in seconds. Their bodies had barely hit the ground before the wall exploded, throwing Styles across the chamber. Still conscious, and desperate to reach the detonator, she dragged herself back towards the console under a barrage of laser fire through the smoking gap in the wall. With blood pouring from her head, Styles pulled herself up to face the console. Almost there, her hand reached for the detonator just as a grenade exploded behind her left ear.

The mess was terrible.

Somewhere in the corridors of the *Vipod Mor*, Mercer heard the explosion. He couldn't know for certain but he sensed it had to do with the Self-Destruct Chamber. As Mercer and Turlough were still alive, the assumption had to be that the chamber had been broken into. If that were so, the crew would have been overrun and killed. Mercer took out his radio and tried to connect to Styles, but there was no reply. Instead there was a text message from Zena:

'Heavy attack all us dead'

Turlough supposed that this was not a time to comment on the sender's poor grammar. 'I'm sorry,' he told Mercer, 'that your friends are dead.'

Mercer closed his eyes. 'There's got to be a way to avenge them.'

'By throwing away your life, and mine with it?' Turlough shook his head. 'You've done everything possible. Come back with me through the time corridor.'

As the smoke began to settle, one of Lytton's Troopers entered the chamber and powered down the Self-Destruct mechanism. For the time being, the facility was safe.

During the skirmish, the Alpha Dalek had arrived. Although keeping a safe distance from the fighting, it was ready to reprimand Lytton for poor strategy and placing the Dalek plan at risk.

Lytton wasn't impressed. 'We won,' he argued. 'That's all that matters.'

'Davros could have been harmed,' Alpha grated.

'Of course he could,' Lytton agreed. 'He should have been removed from the *Vipod Mor* right at the start and taken on board the Dalek battlecruiser. But you couldn't make him?'

'Insolence will not be tolerated!' The Dalek twitched in anger and raised its gun arm.

Lytton knew he'd gone too far. 'I merely meant,' he said quickly, 'that if Alpha Dalek could not succeed, how could I presume even to try?'

Alpha watched him. 'The space station was almost destroyed,' it gurgled. 'I shall report this to the Supreme Dalek.' Alpha turned and left, humming to itself. Lytton's show of humility had left it satisfied ... for now.

Professor Laird was not happy. The lumps and bumps, inflicted earlier by Archer, throbbed painfully. Now, in the warehouse on the time corridor level, she was being held roughly by one of the solders.

Archer and Calder emerged from the gloom pushing Tegan into the area.

'I did try,' Tegan murmured. 'I couldn't find anyone to help.'

Laird couldn't contain herself. 'They're going to send us to the Dalek ship. What sort of living hell will that be?'

'Enough,' said Archer. 'Get them into the time corridor.'

Laird knew she had nothing to lose. She seized the moment and scraped the heel of her boot down the shin of the soldier holding her. The action had the desired effect as he released his grip. She ran. She could do what Tegan couldn't. She could escape.

She was fast too. Laird had almost reached the door by the time Archer drew his sidearm and shot her dead.

Lashing out at Archer, Tegan was dragged by the two soldiers towards the entrance of the time corridor. A moment later, she was tumbling and rolling through time and space.

The Doctor was fully connected to the duplicating machine. It was simply now a matter of setting the coordinates so his personal software could be run. The elaborate process would involve painfully extracting and then transferring his memories, experiences and knowledge to a life-support system before moving them permanently to a Dalek-controlled lookalike husk. Given how old the Time Lord was, this would take quite some time.

Stien had become strangely remote. 'You know you are being processed for special use by Davros?'

The faintest of smiles crossed the Doctor's face. 'Then I should get the best of treatments, the finest of wines and the wittiest of conversation.'

'Are you ready, old boy?'

'You ask as though I have a choice,' said the Doctor.

Suddenly Stien erupted, like a wild seething volcano. '*Choice!*' he snapped. 'Everyone has *choice*! It's in the c-c-c-constitution.' Stien had started to stutter again. 'Twenty-fifth amendment … Or-or-or is it the twenty-sixth? Didn't you g-g-go to school?'

'I must have played truant that day. Or perhaps we didn't go to the same school. Which one did you go to?'

'I c-c-can't remember.'

'Concentrate!' the Doctor urged him. 'You can resist the effects of your duplication, access the areas of your mind shut off by the Dalek control.'

But Stien's confused manner stopped as quickly as it had started. 'I must continue my work,' he said, pulling a small lever on the console. 'I must obey.'

'You must resist!'

But Stien's sudden show of his real self was over and he was now quite zombie-like.

*

To protect other Daleks, the cylinder of the deadly Movellan virus had been loaded into a gas-proof glove box in Davros' laboratory. Kiston and the chemist immediately started to work on it, analysing its structure.

As the Troopers who delivered the cylinder turned to go, Kiston came up behind them and swiftly injected the conditioning formula into their necks.

Davros quietly purred. He now had added more soldiers to his team.

'You must show your loyalty,' he said to the new recruits. 'You must enlist the comrades who escorted you here.'

'We obey.'

It was music to Davros's ears.

And so it continued …

As did the images on a huge Z-ray screen in the Duplication Room. These were being harvested from the Doctor's mind.

From the fifth's Doctor's life, there was the face of Adric, the young man who had died attempting to save Earth and its inhabitants. The memory was painful, as was the sense of guilt. It haunted the Doctor like a sadistic ghost savagely invading his most fragile essence. He always believed he should have done more to save the young man. Instead, Adric died alone and afraid aboard a freighter as it crashed into Earth. This memory forced him to confront the fact that he had never really come to terms with what happened. He had allowed it to be buried deep down in his subconscious.

Another image seeped into his mind as he remembered the Terileptils. Not particularly agreeable creatures, they were nevertheless primarily looking for a way to survive, like everything else in the universe. With their great interest in art and design, it wouldn't have hurt him to guide them back to their own planet, instead of allowing them to be consumed in the Great Fire of London in 1666.

It is said that Time Lords do not experience self-reproach but the Doctor certainly did.

Then came the images of his previous self. A long scarf, a floppy hat and even floppier hair. This was the regeneration who could calm a Dalek with a jelly baby, outthink the sharpest of Cybermen and defeat the most intelligent of creatures. Like other Time Lords he could be eccentric, but he could also be insightful, kind and gentle. The Dalek sensors struggled to process such eccentric emotions, but they knew their duplicate must have all the traits of the original – traits that would kindle trust and familiarity, while the Dalek intelligence behind took hold.

The Doctor writhed and struggled as the macabre procedure continued. He then let out a long terrible scream which echoed and bellowed around the room.

The cry seemed to touch a long-forgotten nerve in Stien's psyche. 'I know how you feel, Doctor,' he sobbed.

The Time Lord continued to scream. 'Please, you're destroying my mind. Recite the amendments. Remember your past!'

Stien wiped his eyes. 'I must do my duty.'

*

All was calm in Davros's laboratory.

With his hands in the gas-proof glove box, the chemist very carefully transferred some of the Movellan virus from the cylinder to a smaller vessel, his every move observed closely by Davros who was enjoying the minutiae of the procedure as any scientist would.

Kiston, who was at the console, turned to Davros. 'The Daleks have secured the Self-Destruct Chamber. The Station is safe.'

'Excellent,' Davros purred.

'The Daleks have also apprehended the Doctor.'

'Better still. He must be brought to me at once,' Davros's voice rattled. 'I have waited a long time for this.' With work advancing well, he saw his dark plan being realised and, unable to contain himself, his rant reverberated around the room: 'I shall build a new race of Daleks. They will be even more deadly … *And I, Davros, shall be their leader.*

'This time we shall triumph!

'My Daleks shall once more become the supreme beings!'

Dazed by the painful journey through the time corridor from Earth, Tegan shuffled into the reception area escorted by a Trooper. At that very same moment, Mercer also entered, followed by Turlough. Seeing the Trooper, Mercer instantly shot him dead and turned his weapon on Tegan.

'Not her,' Turlough said quickly. 'This is Tegan, she's a friend.'

'Pick up that rifle,' said Mercer coldly. 'Remember, it's only for protection.'

'Turlough.' Tegan managed a smile. 'Who's your friend?'

'Talk later,' Mercer insisted. 'We must get away before the Daleks arrive.'

Tegan was suddenly alert. 'And the Doctor?' She pointed at the TARDIS, all ramshackle and half-lurking in an alcove.

'He's here?' Turlough realised. 'If we can get inside the TARDIS, we'll be safe.'

'We must find the Doctor,' Tegan insisted. 'If these Dalek things have him ...'

'We can't stay here in any case.' Mercer grabbed Tegan's hand and pulled her on through the corridor. 'We can talk strategy and about the Doctor there.'

With Turlough following, they started to run.

On a screen in the laboratory, Davros watched Tegan, Turlough and Mercer leave the reception area. The day had just got even better. His spindly finger then moved the camera control stick and it panned across to the area to where the TARDIS was carelessly parked.

'Perfect,' he drooled.

Kiston seemed impressed too. 'Soon the TARDIS will be yours, master.'

Davros nodded. 'Order my Daleks to be dispatched.'

Kiston bowed. 'I obey, master, I obey.'

Strapped down in the Duplication Chamber, the Doctor was writhing in agony as more images extracted from his mind appeared on the Z-ray screen.

This time it was further back in the Time Lord's history. A dark mop of hair, black jacket and checked trousers topped with a whimsical expression. However, mining memories from his second incarnation was too excruciating. It was as though an assassin's blade had gouged too deeply into his psyche.

The experience proved too much and he screamed, and he screamed, *and he screamed.*

Surprisingly, his torment seemed to act as a catalyst, jolting Stien back into some vestige of his original self. 'I can't go on!' he shouted. 'The confusion in my mind is too strong.'

'Quickly, release me,' demanded the Doctor. Reluctantly, Stien struggled to undo the wrist straps.

Unfortunately, the Troopers in the room also saw what was happening. As they moved to restrain the Doctor, Stien slid a small laser pistol from his sleeve. 'Stay back,' he shouted waving the gun in their direction. 'Drop your weapons.'

Lytton entered the bridge of the battlecruiser and reported strong resistance from the east wing on the *Vipod Mor.*

'Dalek casualties will not be tolerated,' the Supreme Dalek retorted. 'More troopers must be duplicated to handle the situation.'

Lytton understood that the Daleks, defeated in war, were paranoid about their numbers dwindling further. Nevertheless, he was not convinced. 'Reports suggest that the duplication process is erratic.'

Alpha bristled. 'The fault is not with Dalek technology but with inferior human minds.'

'Memories are seeping back into the soldiers' consciousness,' Lytton persisted, 'making them unstable and therefore not reliable.'

'A minor problem,' declared the Supreme Dalek.

Lytton refused to be cowed. 'If things go wrong, you could finish up with a mutiny and the loss of your entire fighting force.'

Elsewhere on the battlecruiser, the trio flipped and flopped to avoid Dalek patrols. Beckoned by Turlough, they entered the antechamber leading to the Duplication Chamber. 'I was here earlier,' he said opening the door. 'Be careful. There may still be bodies.'

With the connecting door open, they entered and found, as predicted, several corpses. Taking the initiative, Tegan bent down and identified them as the soldiers from the warehouse. 'This is so sad,' she said. 'Lives taken for no purpose.' She walked across to the Duplication Chamber door. 'I don't know how much more I can stand of this, Turlough.' He looked embarrassed. 'Nowadays there seems to be so much violence in our so-called adventures.'

On the other side of the door, in the actual Duplication Chamber itself, the Doctor and Stien, both still groggy, had started to tie up the two Troopers with wire from the electrodes.

'Now what?' said Stien. 'The Dalek conditioning could c-c-cloud my mind at any moment.'

'You'll be safe in the TARDIS,' the Doctor reassured him.

'But you won't. Under the Dalek influence, I could kill you.'

The Time Lord smiled. 'I'll take the chance.'

Suddenly the connecting door opened to reveal Turlough, Tegan and Mercer.

'*Doctor!*' cried Tegan joyfully.

'Don't just stand there,' the Doctor grumped. 'Help us to tie up these men!'

Tegan crossed to the Time Lord and squatted next to him. 'I see you're back on the old reef knots,' she smiled.

'Save the quips for later,' said Mercer pointing at the flashing red light on the security camera. 'The Daleks know where we are.'

'Indeed,' said the Doctor. 'The Supreme Dalek could be looking at us right now.' He picked up one of the Troopers' laser rifles, pointed it at the security camera and fired, sending the parts scattering across the room. 'That will teach him to be a nosy parker.' He then turned the weapon on the duplication device and fired again. This time, like molten glass being spilt from a massive crucible, the remains of the machine dribbled down the wall, thereby destroying access to the vital information stolen from his mind.

In the corridor, the Beta Dalek heard the gunfire and immediately reacted. In a wild fury, it entered the Duplication Chamber. 'The Supreme Dalek orders you to cease fire,' it squawked. 'You must surrender. This is a Dalek command.'

But, of course, no one was listening. Instead Mercer and the Doctor turned quickly and fired directly, close-range at the Dalek, damaging its eyestalk.

'My vision is impaired. I cannot see. My vision is impaired!' Spinning wildly, it fired blasts of deadly energy.

Tegan threw Turlough to the floor and dived down beside him as the death rays sizzled past.

Mercer jammed his gun against the Dalek's grille and fired round after round into it until it went quiet and stopped still.

'Let's get out of here,' insisted the Doctor grabbing his coat from the floor.

The group rushed out of the Duplication Chamber along the battlecruiser's numerous and interminable corridors towards the reception area where the TARDIS was parked. With quick and alert thinking, they managed to avoid all Daleks and patrolling Troopers.

Their luck held as they raced into the reception area as only one Trooper was on guard. With the briefest of blows from Mercer, the guard fell, unconscious. As this was happening, Tegan threw herself at the door of the TARDIS. Instead of flicking open, as it almost always did, she bounced off it.

IT WAS LOCKED!

For the first time in the history of almost everything, the door had been secured.

Tegan was furious. 'What's the matter with you, Doctor? We have the whole of hell plus Uncle Harry chasing us and you decide to lock the door.'

'You'd rather the TARDIS fell into Dalek hands?' The Doctor rummaged in his pockets. 'The key's here somewhere.'

While he searched, Mercer and Stien, weapons at the ready, moved back to the corridor. Incredibly, no one had followed them.

'It's got to be here somewhere,' the Doctor said, trying to calm Tegan.

Stien was getting nervous. 'C-c-can't you hurry?'

The Doctor continued to ferret in every pocket until there was a light bulb moment. Taking out his folded panama and unfurling it, the key tumbled out.

'A *hat*!' screeched Tegan. 'What numbskull keeps a key in a folded hat?!'

'Whatever you're going to do,' shouted Mercer, 'do it now.'

The Doctor opened the door and the group tumbled in, slamming it behind them. Such was the panic to get in, Mercer didn't even notice that the TARDIS was bigger on the inside than it was on the outside.

The Doctor did his usual pre-flight fiddling on the console.

'Where are we going?' panted Tegan.

'Earth.'

'Best news all year,' Turlough muttered.

With the time rotor oscillating, the Doctor switched on the auto-navigation system. 'Tell me, Stien. Why has Davros been rescued by the Daleks?'

'They need a cure for a virus that has been annihilating them,' said Stien. 'They call it the M-M-Movellan virus.'

'I'm sure Davros will find it for them,' said the Doctor.

Mercer turned to Turlough. 'That cylinder we saw transported to the lab under guard ...'

'They're kept in the warehouse on Earth,' Stien said. 'The cylinders were safer there, and they acted as a lure. With the Bomb Disposal Squad duplicated, the Daleks had people to guard the warehouse who wouldn't arouse suspicion.'

The Doctor nodded, pondering. 'I am going outside now, and may be gone some time.'

Tegan caught the Doctor's arm as he crossed to the door. 'Never mind the cod history quotes, where are you going?'

The Doctor said matter-of-factly, 'To kill Davros.'

Tegan was horrified. 'Doctor ...!'

'I must,' the Doctor said quietly. 'Davros created the Daleks. He must not be allowed to save them. If they are dying of the virus, so be it.'

Tegan squirmed. 'But murder?'

'Once before I held back from destroying the Daleks,' he added. 'It was a mistake I do not intend to repeat. Davros must die!'

The room fell silent whilst the group assessed the implication of the Doctor's decision and how it might affect them.

'Count me in,' said Mercer. 'Because of Davros, nearly all my colleagues are dead.'

'I wouldn't mind a taste of revenge,' added Stien.

'No,' cried Tegan. 'Doctor, you can't do this. This isn't your style at all ...'

Ignoring Tegan's response, the Time Lord said, 'Wait as long as you can, but should the Daleks attack, leave at once.'

Accompanied by Mercer and Stien, the Doctor left the TARDIS for a fate unknown.

Uncharacteristically, Turlough placed his arm around Tegan's shoulder. 'The Doctor will be back.'

Suddenly, Tegan welled up. 'It's not whether he'll be back, it's what he's about to do. *This is murder!*'

Tegan was right. But when it came to murder, Davros was the ultimate exponent.

Chapter Ten

In his laboratory, the Creator of the Daleks was triumphant, holding up a small container of the Movellan virus, recently decanted by Kiston. 'With the aid of this,' he gloated, 'I shall reclaim my rightful place as leader of the Daleks.' Davros glared ferociously around the room. 'I presume there are no dissenters?'

Strangely enough, there weren't.

Lytton, on the other hand, was less jubilant. Seeing the destruction in the Duplication Chamber, his mood hardened. To add insult to injury, two of his Troopers had been trussed up like wild speelsnapes, their limbs retained by neat double reef knots.

His professionalism as an elite soldier had been compromised. This should never have happened.

'We must find the Doctor,' he said. 'I need to make an example of him.'

In a corridor on the *Vipod Mor,* Stien appeared to be escorting the Time Lord and Mercer as if they were prisoners.

On a security screen, Davros could see the group. 'Could this be the Doctor?' It had been many years since their last encounter and the Time Lord could have regenerated.

'The uniformed man is Stien,' Kiston confirmed, 'a member of Lytton's Elite Guard. He would never be assigned to escort duties unless the prisoner was very important.'

'The Doctor and his TARDIS …' Davros licked his shrivelled lips. '*Perfect.*'

Meanwhile, Lytton had arrived in the battlecruiser's reception area in search of the Doctor. After trying to enter the TARDIS unsuccessfully, he instructed two of his Troopers to stand guard.

'Anyone who comes near or tries to leave this vessel, apprehend them at once.'

And with the remainder of his men, he moved on in search of the elusive Time Lord.

Having seen the Troopers on the screen outside the TARDIS, Turlough insisted they dematerialise at once.

'No. We wait,' said Tegan.

'May I remind you, the Doctor said we should go if the TARDIS was threatened,' Turlough said. 'He even preset the controls!'

'*No!*' Tegan insisted. 'The Doctor said we go *only* if the TARDIS is attacked.'

Outside the TARDIS, the conditioned Daleks had entered the reception area, seeking to secure the time machine for Davros. Lytton's two Troopers on guard were instantly destroyed by a withering blast of Dalek gunfire.

'Davros's orders must be obeyed,' chanted the Epsilon Dalek. 'We must find a way of entering.'

The Gamma Dalek opened fire on the TARDIS. The blue police box shell glowed negative under the attack, but the doors remained secure.

For the time being, Tegan and Turlough were safe inside.

From the battlecruiser's bridge, the Supreme Dalek had watched these events unfold on a screen.

'The Daleks in the reception area do not respond to my instructions,' screeched the Alpha Dalek. 'They have been conditioned. It is the work of Davros.'

'He is unreliable,' said the Supreme Dalek. 'He cannot be trusted and must be destroyed.'

Menacingly Alpha edged closer. 'And the rogue Daleks?'

'They must be captured and reprogrammed.' The Supreme's voice grew louder and more aggressive in tone. 'Nothing, not even Davros, can be allowed to stand in the way of the Dalek masterplan!'

As Lytton and his men continued their way through the battlecruiser, he received the order from the Supreme Dalek that

Davros must be eradicated. He had become too dangerous to be left at large. It had always been a risk that Davros would follow his own agenda in an attempt to gain total power. The work he had undertaken on the virus would have to suffice in furthering the Dalek cause.

Lytton instructed two men to carry out the order. 'I'm going back to the reception area,' said Lytton. 'Should the Doctor try to return to his ship, I want to be there to greet him.'

So it goes.

The Doctor, Stien and Mercer finally arrived at Davros's laboratory. Still maintaining the pretence of prisoner and escort, they entered the area.

On seeing the Doctor, Davros's face contorted into a complete look of repugnance. 'I have waited many years for this meeting.'

'I'm sorry to have detained you,' replied the Doctor.

'It was but a pleasure deferred. Now you are here, you will repay ten-fold for the mental agony I have suffered.'

In the background, Kiston and the chemist continued their work with the Movellan virus.

'There's one thing I'll say for you, Davros. Your conversation is utterly predictable. You're like a deranged child. Always talk of revenge, killing and destruction.'

Davros grimaced. 'It is the only path to ultimate power.'

'But to what end? Just more suffering for those unfortunate enough to survive.'

'Only for those who resist my will.'

The Doctor extended his hand towards Mercer who placed a laser rifle in it.

'What are you doing?' Davros demanded urgently.

The Doctor felt the weight of the gun and switched it to kill. 'Until I walked through that door,' he said, 'I foolishly hoped you had changed enough for me not to have to do this.'

'Stien, kill him,' Davros ordered. But the man with a stutter remained perfectly still.

'You don't seem to understand, I'm not here as your prisoner, Davros,' said the Time Lord, 'but your executioner.'

Davros's parched lips quivered. 'Kill me and you will release the full power of the Daleks.'

The Doctor smiled. 'It's not what I hear. They say the Daleks are a spent force, that they're dying.'

'There are other Dalek nations scattered throughout the universe. We will succeed. Find the cure.'

'After I've dealt with you,' said the Doctor, 'I shall find and destroy them all. They will not succeed.'

'I think not . . .' said Davros. 'But with my help you just might.'

'Help?' The Doctor was surprised by the word.

'You, in your way, are not an unambitious man. Like me, you are a renegade.'

'Save your breath.'

'I had planned to completely redesign the Daleks. Kiston will confirm what I am saying is true.'

Kiston looked up. 'It is so.'

'My mistake was making them totally ruthless,' said Davros. 'It restricted their ability to cope with creatures who not only rely on logic, but also instinct and intuition. That is a factor I will correct.'

'And compassion? Are they to be programmed for that?'

'They will learn to recognise the strength that can be drawn from such an emotion.'

'But only to make the Daleks more efficient killers?'

'No, to make them a more positive force.'

'For destruction!'

'The universe is at war, Doctor. Name one planet whose history is not littered with atrocities and ambition for empire. It is a universal way of life.'

'Which I do not accept,' was the Doctor's emphatic response.

'I am offering you a foot in reality. Join me and you will have total power at the head of a new Dalek army.'

But before the Time Lord could reply, Stien indicated the screen showing two Troopers in the corridor outside.

' Deal with them,' said the Doctor. Stien and Mercer left.

'To be honest,' said the Doctor, 'I wouldn't know what to do with an army...'

He raised the laser rifle.

With the sound of lasers from Davros's Daleks pounding the door of the TARDIS, Tegan and Turlough were also in disagreement.

She had tried to reassure him that the time machine was resilient and had survived many attacks before. He might have been happier if the TARDIS had an armoury, but it didn't.

As he lamented this absence, a howl came from the console and the time machine groaned and moaned and then dematerialised.

'It can't be the Daleks,' Tegan said.

'The Doctor must have preset the controls on the timer,' Turlough realised.

Tegan felt her stomach turn. 'He didn't intend to return.'

Suddenly, the floor beneath them rose by forty-five degrees, leaving them hanging from the console.

'We've entered the Dalek time corridor,' shouted Turlough. 'We're going back to the warehouse!' He pulled at the various controls on the console in an attempt to initiate the override and pull free, but he failed.

Meanwhile on the bridge in the battlecruiser, the Supreme Dalek turned towards Alpha as it approached.

'Sensors show the time corridor is being used by Davros's Daleks,' Alpha reported. 'They are following the Doctor's TARDIS to Earth.'

'Let them go,' the Supreme gushed. 'In due course, they will serve my greater purpose.'

In the laboratory, the tension was rising. The Doctor stood before Davros, his gun aimed squarely at his head. The confrontation had now caught the attention of Kiston and the chemist, who had stopped their various activities.

'You hesitate, Doctor,' said Davros. 'If I were you, I would be dead.'

'I lack your practice.'

'You are soft, Time Lord. You prefer to stand and watch. Action requires courage, something you lack.'

The mood outside the laboratory was equally edgy. Stien tried to order the two guards away, but began stammering helplessly. Fearing the Troopers were about to open fire, Mercer raised his gun and shot them. Hoping for a sense of retribution, all he felt was a sense of despair and physical sickness. Yet another mistake in his disastrous command.

'W-w-what do we do with the bodies?' asked Stien.

'What's the matter with you?' Mercer was concerned by the return of Stien's stammer.

'The Dalek conditioning ... It's st-st-starting to take hold again.'

A boot scuffed the floor further up the corridor. 'Drop your guns,' echoed the voice from the darkness as three Troopers stepped forward.

'It's all right,' said Stien with a smile. 'They're our Troopers.'

Mercer stared at him in horror. 'They're *Dalek* Troopers!' He opened fire, killing the first soldier. But the remaining two shot back, and Mercer's brain burst inside his skull. He dropped to his knees and pitched forward onto his face.

Horrified by the killings, Stien fired wildly, destroying another Trooper. He was not so fortunate with the third soldier, who returned fire and wounded him.

Having heard the commotion outside, fearing for his friends, the Doctor backed away from Davros and opened the door. In front of him, an armed Trooper stood over Stien. Having been distracted by the door's sudden movement, the soldier turned to face the Doctor, bringing up his gun. As he did, Stien fired from his prone position and killed him.

Seeing Mercer was dead, the Doctor ran to Stien whose injured left arm was now oozing blood.

With surprising speed, Stien grabbed his laser pistol from the floor and aimed it at the Doctor. 'Stay where you are,' he said climbing to his feet. 'I can't control my mind. I'm not safe.'

'You need medical attention,' the Doctor began.

'I caused Mercer's death.' Stien staggered away further up the dark corridor. 'Don't follow me … I m-m-may be forced to kill you. The Dalek c-c-conditioning is getting stronger again.'

At that moment, the door to the laboratory was slammed shut by Kiston, locking the Doctor out of the room. 'I'm an imbecile!' he muttered to himself as he kicked the door hard. 'There must be a way in …' He threw his shoulder against the door but it didn't give. If only he'd had the sonic screwdriver, he knew he would have gained access in a flash. But his various attempts failed. Aware that more Troopers would be drawn here in moments, the dejected Doctor moved away.

Inside the laboratory, Davros watched as the Doctor shuffled away, the faintest of smiles on his lips.

'Shall I go after him?' said Kiston.

Davros pondered for a second. 'No, our work here is more important.'

'The Daleks will investigate the gunfire.'

'Then it is all the more important we are prepared for them. The Supreme Dalek's plan must not succeed!'

For the Doctor, it was proving harder to get back to the reception area on the battlecruiser. Dodging Trooper patrols and having to find his way around bulkhead doors inconveniently sealed for security purposes, he was forced further into the *Vipod Mor* and away from the entrance to the time corridor, and Tegan and Turlough.

If only he had his TARDIS, he thought.

But that was materialising, with its attendant groans and moans, in the warehouse at Shad Thames.

Inside the console room, Tegan activated the scanner screen and saw they were back in the basement near to where the cylinders had been discovered. Highly distressed, she was concerned as to how the Doctor would get back without his TARDIS.

In the reception area, anticipating the Doctor, Lytton heard the buzz of his radio. From the other end came the angry voice of the Supreme Dalek.

'Your Troopers have failed. Davros still lives.'

'He's a hard man to kill,' said Lytton. 'I sent my best men. Why not just shoot down the *Vipod Mor*? Kill Davros and everything on board.'

'I must see him dead,' the Supreme Dalek seethed. 'I have dispatched Daleks to complete the task you failed. You must redeem yourself. You must destroy Davros's Daleks.'

'I thought you wanted them alive?' said Lytton. That you wanted to avoid more Dalek casualties.'

'The rogue units are no longer contained. They have followed the TARDIS to Earth. Possession of the TARDIS will give Davros an unacceptable advantage. They must be exterminated.'

'And what of the duplicates in the warehouse?' said Lytton.

'They are armed only with primitive human weapons. They will die.'

Lytton switched off his radio, contemplating the Supreme's reprimand. He knew this was a mission that he might not survive.

Hearing of Lytton's mission to Earth, and probable death, pleased the Alpha Dalek exceedingly. But what pleased it more was its belief that the Supreme Dalek had made an error of judgement.

'Should Lytton survive,' it prattled, 'there is a risk that he will use the Movellan virus against us.'

Angered that Alpha had raised something it hadn't considered, the Supreme Dalek snapped back, 'The cylinders must be retrieved and returned for safekeeping on board the battlecruiser. Organise immediately!'

Reluctantly the Alpha Dalek said 'I obey.'

*

The sepulchral gloom of the long dark corridor matched Stien's own demoralised frame of mind. Holding his arm and slumped against a wall, the pain had become nearly unbearable.

As he reasoned and argued with himself to be more positive, it came into his mind that he must find and use the Self-Destruct Chamber.

It would be his one and only chance to defeat Davros and the Supreme Dalek.

Summoning what was left of his energy, he staggered on, much in the way Tegan was doing in the warehouse at Shad Thames.

Emerging from the TARDIS, followed by Turlough, Tegan made her way to where the cylinders were stored. She knew their only chance of defeating the Daleks was by releasing the deadly contents.

But how to do it?

'Professor Laird and the soldiers spent two days trying to break into a cylinder with no luck.' Tegan carefully lifted a cylinder and was surprised by how light it was. 'How are we going to succeed where they failed?'

'You mean succeed in unleashing an alien plague upon the Earth? This is lunacy.'

Tegan turned from Turlough, heading back to the TARDIS with the cylinder, just as an incredible electronic buzz tore at her ears.

'Look.' Turlough pointed as the remaining cylinders in the trench slowly disappeared.

Gone home to Mummy, Tegan thought.

Upstairs in the warehouse, Archer, Calder and the two soldiers who had been duplicated to serve the Supreme Dalek watched the arrival of Davros's small but heavily armed fighting force. Their order to destroy them was absurd, as they were not equipped with suitable weaponry.

'What do we do, sir?' asked Calder.

'It seems,' Archer said sadly, 'we die with dignity.'

And with that, Davros's Daleks opened and destroyed them instantly.

In the reception area on the battlecruiser, Lytton and his troopers readied themselves to fight. Heavily armed with an assortment of weapons, they prepared to travel to Earth.

'Let's go,' he snapped.

Without questioning, the soldiers entered the time corridor and were gone.

Kiston and the chemist had packed the small phials of the deadly Movellan virus into a field satchel.

'Go,' ordered Davros. 'The Supreme must be moving against us by now. Release the virus in the Daleks' battlecruiser.'

Meanwhile, the fragile peace of the warehouse was broken again as Lytton and his team began to emerge from the time corridor.

Davros's rogue Daleks glided forward immediately and opened fire.

Lytton dived to the floor. 'Take cover!' he roared and returned a burst of shots from his laser rifle. This allowed his Troopers to disperse themselves amongst the boxes and debris.

From the safety of his hiding place near the Self-Destruct Chamber, Stien could see two Troopers on guard.

He had to remove them but, with his arm frozen by pain and barely able to walk, this would prove very difficult. He would need to summon up every gram of concentration he had to carry out his task.

In the reception area of the battlecruiser, the Alpha Dalek watched as the cylinders of Movellan virus were carried away by troopers. Alpha had decided it would lead a sortie to Earth and fulfil the Supreme Dalek's commands.

'Proceed,' it ordered. 'Everything in the warehouse must be exterminated – including Lytton and his troops.'

'We obey,' came the expected chorus.

As the Daleks dissolved in the time corridor, the Doctor popped his head around the door of the reception area. 'Just in time,' he muttered as the Daleks disappeared.

Noticing two flat-pack grenades by the machine pistol rack, the Doctor swiftly picked them up and moved to the time corridor entrance. 'Here we go again,' he said, stepping into the void. He did not see a sleek black cat stealthily follow him into the tunnel.

Soon they were both sent rumbling, bumbling and tumbling towards Earth.

On board the *Vipod Mor*, Kiston and the chemist were proceeding towards the battlecruiser when they ran straight into the rapid fire of two Daleks. The chemist was killed instantly. Kiston fell and, although wounded, managed to pull a phial of the Movellan virus from the satchel. Before he could break the seal, the Daleks fired again and he died.

Davros's plans had taken a setback.

The battle in the warehouse continued with the deafening noise of laser fire. The superior gun power of Davros's Daleks was too much for Lytton's Troopers, and one by one they died.

Lytton lay motionless, very still, feigning death ...

Then slowly he opened his right eye and scanned the area in front of him.

Unseen by the two guards outside the Self-Destruct Chamber, it was now-or-never time for Stien. Checking his rifle, he mentally braced himself, then rushed forward, firing as he went. To his amazement, the two guards fell dead without so much as a whimper.

With great effort, Stien half ran and half stumbled into the Self-Destruct Chamber, ready for any trouble he might encounter.

On finding the area empty, he managed a small smile. For the first time in what felt like a lifetime he had achieved something, Something for himself.

It was just a pity so many people had to die as a result of what would happen next.

There was now a sinister calm in the warehouse. Gamma Dalek was cautiously checking for any signs of life among the enemy casualties, ready to exterminate.

'We must find the TARDIS,' Delta Dalek ordered. 'That is our prime mission. We must obey Davros.'

No sooner had the command been given, than the squad commanded by the Alpha Dalek formed in the entrance to the time corridor.

'What is happening?' Gamma asked Delta.

'The Supreme Dalek wishes us destroyed,' said Delta, gliding backwards into the shadows. 'These Daleks must be exterminated!'

Gamma hid behind the rubble of a dividing wall as Alpha's force fanned out into the warehouse. 'We must find the traitors,' he ordered. 'Our enemies must be destroyed.'

'No!' shouted the Gamma Dalek as it emerged from the shadows. 'We are not traitors. We simply serve our Creator.'

'You blaspheme. The Supreme Dalek is your ruler. Its – *our* – diktats must be obeyed at all times.'

'Davros must be honoured,' Gamma insisted.

'He must be exterminated,' Alpha spat.

As so often in the Dalek world, there was a horrendous point of disagreement. What with one claiming the Supreme Dalek as their ruler and the other Davros, there could only be one outcome.

Confronting each other like two sociopathic prima donnas, the two Daleks turned their relentless firepower on each other and exploded in twin balls of fire.

The remaining Daleks anxiously swirled around, seeking cover, instructions, vengeance. And so they missed another significant development as the time corridor's exit glowed once again.

The Doctor was back in town.

Chapter Eleven

The Supreme Dalek registered the death of Alpha without emotion – but a second later felt a wave of intense hatred at the sight of Stien on his screen. The duplicate was beginning to activate the Self-Destruct device.

'Daleks to the Self-Destruct Chamber,' screamed the Supreme Dalek. 'A hostile has broken in. Emergency! Emergency! He must be stopped. He must be *exterminated*!'

After the destruction of the Alpha and Gamma Daleks, a major skirmish broke out. Two tribal groups of Daleks fighting to the bitter end for supremacy, neither side knowing quite where they would finish up with their loyalty.

That's Daleks for you.

Amidst the deafening salvo, the Doctor left the time corridor, followed by the cat. They both darted across the warehouse until they found an uncertain safety behind a heap of debris. 'It's times like these that you wished you'd worn your flak jacket,' said the Doctor, stroking the cat.

'I wish they made them in my size,' replied the feline matter-of-factly.

Before the Doctor could react, yet another salvo echoed and the cat was gone, leaving the Time Lord wondering whether he had really heard what he thought he'd heard or if it was just the lingering effects of the Daleks' mental probing.

It was obviously one of those days.

Jolted back to the real world by the sight of a Dalek gliding past, the Doctor quickly attached one of Lytton's high-power grenades to its casing. A few moments later, the Dalek exploded into an inferno, the mutant, trapped in its casing, flailing and bubbling. This gave the Doctor time to run to the stairs. On reaching them, another Dalek loomed into view. Prepared, the Doctor bowled a second grenade and destroyed it. The blast threw him to the filthy floor, where for a second he made eye contact with a figure in the shadows. It was Lytton, weapon in hand, who immediately fired at the Doctor. Quickly, the Time Lord slithered down the stairs and out of range.

Reaching the floor below, the Doctor saw the welcome blue bulk of the TARDIS. He charged through its doors and almost fell over Tegan who was on the floor examining the cylinder.

'Doctor!' She stared in shock, then beamed.

'Well done, Tegan!' the Doctor said, indicating the cylinder.

Turlough was less enthusiastic. 'I warned her that if she opened it, the Movellan virus could start an epidemic.'

The Doctor calmed him: 'The virus is only partial to Daleks. It will die once it's done its work.'

Tegan stood up and placed the cylinder on the console.

'Lunch has arrived for our friend here,' said the Doctor patting the cylinder. 'I think it's time it was served to our guests.'

He then activated the time rotor, did some careful calculations and sent the TARDIS up one storey in the warehouse, just like a lift in Henrik's.

On the *Vipod Mor*, on a security screen, Davros saw two Daleks making their way towards his laboratory.

Quietly, he moved to a portal set in the wall and opened it to reveal an escape pod which he primed ready for departure. He then operated a switch on the console of his chariot and a panel slid back, showing several phials of Movellan virus. Wasting no time, he broke two open and threw them towards the door. As he did, the door was blown open.

Two Daleks entered.

'I did not summon you,' Davros said calmly.

'The Supreme Dalek orders your death,' said one of the Daleks.

'We are here to exterminate you,' said the other.

'You have been betrayed,' said Davros. 'The Supreme Dalek intends to destroy you with the Movellan virus.'

'Our destruction is unimportant.'

'Then you abandon your existence without purpose. Why not join me? I will make you rulers of the universe.'

As he continued with his tissue of lies, smoke began to billow from the two Daleks. 'What is happening?' they demanded.

'You said it yourselves.' Davros's face cracked into a crinkly grin. 'Your destruction is unimportant …'

The TARDIS had materialised, the time rotor was stationary. Checking the scanner screen, they found the Daleks had stopped fighting.

Picking up the cylinder, the Doctor flipped open an almost invisible panel and turned on a small valve.

'So that's how you open it!' said a relieved Tegan.

Turlough operated the door mechanism, and the Time Lord edged outside and gingerly slid the cylinder along the floor into the warehouse.

He then popped his head out and saw through the smoky atmosphere Lytton, still alive in a gloomy corner. Somehow, he had changed his uniform, and was now dressed in the style of a twentieth-century Earth police inspector – albeit one armed with a laser rifle. Lytton fired at the Doctor who quickly ducked back inside the TARDIS and slammed the door.

A gentle hiss began to escape from the cylinder and death began to spread its fingers across the warehouse.

The Doctor joined his companions at the console. 'So,' asked Turlough, 'how long before the virus does its work?'

'Well ...' The Doctor sounded uncertain. 'The Movellan virus is terribly efficient. It will attack them almost immediately ... I hope.'

In Davros's laboratory, the immediate effects of the virus on the infected Daleks were well under way.

Davros watched them with absolute concentration. This was, after all, an important experiment for him. Billowing and oozing from various orifices, vast amounts of froth and other debris came from the Daleks' casings. They were both screaming in excruciating pain. It was a horrible spectacle.

He smiled tenderly. Even in death, his creations served him well.

In the warehouse at Shad Thames, Dalek screams could be heard again as the cylinder continued to hiss like a very angry cat – one in a flak jacket that fitted well.

With speed, a Trooper sprinted across the floor, followed by a flash from a Dalek gun stick which wildly missed its target.

'What is happening?' Smoke billowed from under the Dalek's dome as it slurred its speech. 'I cannot see. My vision is impaired ...'

Just as with the Daleks in Davros's laboratory, smoke was joined by a froth-like substance spurting and oozing from its casing. The Dalek let out a last, hideous scream and died.

Unperturbed by the scene, Lytton vanished into the shadows, topping his police uniform with a peaked cap pulled from under his jacket.

*

A riot of lights radiated from the console in the Self-Destruct Chamber.

'Done it.' Stien said breathlessly. 'Must rest.' His voice was now faint. 'So tired.' He sighed and slumped down.

Not far away, Davros had finished recording his observations of the Daleks' destruction. Now, in victorious tone, he exclaimed, 'The Daleks are dead. *Long live the new Daleks!*'

But his triumphant mood came to a sudden end as smoke wafted from his console and the now familiar froth oozed from every seam of his chariot. His whole body felt horribly overheated and he flung out his single arm as if hoping to protect it.

'No! It can't be!' he squealed horribly. 'I am not a Dalek!'

Stretching his arm towards the escape hatch, He was defiant. 'I cannot die! *I am Davros!*

'I AM DAVROS!

'I AM NOT A DALEK!'

The warfare had ceased in the warehouse, but the torment of the decaying and screaming Daleks was hideous, sending ghostly echoes around the building.

In the TARDIS, the Doctor, Tegan and Turlough watched the Dalek suffering on the screen in the console room. Shocked and sickened by all she had witnessed, Tegan looked away.

The Doctor's voice was little more than a whisper. 'It's over.'

'It was horrible,' Tegan said. Turlough nodded in agreement.

'The Earth is safe,' reasoned the Doctor. 'At least until the Daleks find an antidote for the Movellan virus.'

Suddenly the screen flickered and the image changed. Now it showed the Supreme Dalek, transmitting from a secret location. 'You have not won, Doctor.'

The Time Lord was defiant. 'You won't be able to invade Earth.'

'There is no need to invade. You forget, Doctor. I have my duplicates. Some have already been placed in strategic political and military positions across the planet. The collapse of Earth society will soon occur.'

'No,' screamed Tegan.

'Your duplicates aren't stable,' the Doctor insisted. 'You've been fighting a war on too many fronts – you still have no cure for the Movellan virus, and even had you the numbers, you can't attack Gallifrey without my duplicate.'

'The Daleks will triumph,' the Supreme insisted. 'The Daleks' true destiny is to rule the universe!'

In the Self-Destruct Chamber, Stien found focus and pulled himself to his feet as two Daleks edged their way into the room.

'Hello boys ...' he said mischievously, moving his hand gently towards the destruct button. 'Just in time for the fun.'

The Daleks responded with a barrage of fire. This sent Stien hurtling backwards. Impacting hard against a nearby wall, he was then thrown forward onto the console.

'Sorry, but the ride might be a bit bumpy.' With one last effort, he pulled a lever operating the detonator.

The explosion was horrendous as both the battlecruiser and the *Vipod Mor* were ripped into a trillion tiny shreds.

Having seen the two ships explode, the Doctor moved his hand to a lever and closed the white screen. Tegan was in a state of shock. Turlough just stared blankly. There was no jubilation on board the TARDIS.

'The Dalek ship has been destroyed,' said the Doctor.

'How?' asked Turlough.

The Doctor studied the TARDIS readouts. 'The Self-Destruct device on the *Vipod Mor*.'

'Was it Davros?' Tegan wondered aloud.

'No, no. Stien, I would think.'

'Stien?' Turlough looked surprised. 'But he was a Dalek Trooper.'

'He was originally from Earth. He must have finally decided which side he was on.' And with that, followed by Tegan and Turlough, he left the TARDIS.

With an even tread, Lytton walked along Shad Thames. He stopped as his two policemen stepped from a doorway and both saluted. They then fell into line behind him and proceeded onwards …

It had been a hell of a day, Lytton thought. The fighting had been scrappy, disorganised and too many of his Troopers were dead. Worst of all, he had not achieved his main goal, the real reason for accepting the Supreme Dalek's commission, and that was to bring about the death of the Doctor. Such an action would have raised his kudos to an immeasurable height. *Never mind,* he thought. *Next time.*

There's always a next time.

The remains of the battle were strewn across the warehouse floor, strange alien artefacts left to smoulder in a Victorian edifice. There was an acrid smell, and smoke still rose from some of the destroyed Daleks. It was a picture of total carnage.

'Are you sure all the duplicates are unstable?' asked Tegan.

The Doctor shook his head.

'Then you should inform Earth's authorities,' she said. 'They'll listen to you.'

'This is 1984,' said Turlough. 'You know what they're like when there's talk of alien invasion. They'll just laugh and then lock us in a psychiatric hospital.'

'If you want proof,' said Tegan, 'look around you. It's everywhere. This place is loaded with the stuff.'

'And, of course, there's Lytton,' said Turlough, 'a walking talking living dog of an alien.'

The Doctor looked around. 'Yes, where is he?' he said urgently. 'I saw him earlier. In fact, he tried to kill me.'

'All the best people do,' muttered Tegan.

'More importantly,' said the Doctor, 'he'll know who the duplicates are.'

Tegan wasn't convinced.

'Trust me. He's the sort of man who would make it his business. And all we need to do is find him.' A broad smile spread across the Doctor's face. 'Earth is safe.'

But there was no smile from Tegan, in fact quite the opposite. 'Are you absolutely sure about that?'

The Time Lord was surprised at her response. 'Aren't you pleased?'

'Of course.' Tegan nodded but winced as she looked around the warehouse. 'I think I'm growing tired of all this …'

'What's the matter?'

'A lot of good people have died today …' She sounded tearful. 'And, to be honest, I'm growing sick of it.'

'Do you think I wanted it this way?'

'No, but I don't think I can go on.'

The Doctor looked puzzled. 'You want to stay on Earth?'

Tegan nodded. 'When I became an air stewardess, my aunt Vanessa said that if I stopped enjoying it, I should give it up. I think she was right.' She paused. 'It's stopped being fun, Doctor.' She shook the Doctor's hand, rather formally, and then Turlough's. 'Goodbye. I'll miss you both.'

'Please don't go,' the Doctor said. 'Not like this.'

But Tegan had already turned and was quickly gone.

Turlough turned to the Doctor, looking for some reaction. 'Are you angry?'

The Doctor shrugged. 'It's rather strange,' he said mournfully. 'I left Gallifrey for similar reasons. I'd grown tired of their lifestyle.

It seems I must mend my ways ... or regenerate. But before I do either, we must find Lytton.'

They crossed to the TARDIS and went inside.

Tegan watched from the shadows of the warehouse, her face wet with tears, as the time machine dematerialised.

'Goodbye. Doctor ... I will miss you.'

Coda

The click-clack of heels echoed across the cobble stones of Shad Thames.

It was Tegan.

In a hurry.

As always.

Having just said she didn't want to travel any more with the Doctor, she had stomped out of his life with the barest of farewells. Tegan remembered muttering something about her Aunt Vanessa, not finding life on board the TARDIS fun and how she'd wanted to stay on Earth.

That wasn't much of a farewell.

Tegan and the Doctor had travelled together for three years and he deserved a better explanation for her sudden departure.

But it was too late.

The Time Lord, in his TARDIS, had gone. Probably already on the other side of the universe, involved in yet another escapade, another challenge.

Tegan was now confused.

Had she made the right decision?

There were always adventures, she recalled. Some of them scary, but many of them exuberant, ebullient, and yes, even fun. There were, after all, the many planets she had visited, the amazing civilisations she had encountered, the sheer exhilaration and wonder of travelling throughout the universe. She would never have had such experiences flying for Air Australia.

So, why had she been so negative?

Tegan's mind was in a swirl.

Now she was free of the Doctor, but where was she precisely in time and space? She knew the year and had a vague idea of the day and month, but how would she fit back into the system?

Tegan began to panic.

Would she have been missed?

Would the police have been informed of her absence?

How would she explain her whereabouts for the last three years?

Did she still have somewhere to live?

So many questions.

Tegan's head spun.

As she walked by the derelict Custom Houses, with their ever-so-spooky atmosphere, it started to rain.

That's all she needed. Not only confused and lost, she was now wet through, with rain streaking down her face. Reaching Tower Bridge, she started to climb the stone steps to the bascule level of the main carriageway. As she went, the two policemen, who had carried out such dreadful murders earlier, stepped from a deep warehouse doorway and, unseen by Tegan, started to follow her.

On reaching the carriageway, the first thing Tegan noticed was how few people there were in the area. A major tourist attraction, Tower Bridge, and its accompanying castle, usually commanded a large and constant stream of visitors from all over the world. This was very odd. It was surely too soon for the authorities to have discovered the destroyed Daleks and alien artefacts in the warehouse and cordoned off this part of Bermondsey.

Equally strange was how Tegan was now feeling. She was becoming energised and had acquired an enormous sense of power and self-control. Her mind was less clouded and more focused.

Tegan started to cross the bridge, the Thames lapping and slapping vividly against the flood walls. As she reached the middle of the bridge, having admired along the way the Cornish granite and the fossil-embedded Portland stone, she suddenly saw behind her the two policemen. Her first reaction was of horror. This was rapidly followed by a powerful sense of what she was going to do next.

She ran to the bridge's handrail. There was little activity on the river below apart from a barge covered in heavy canvas chugging towards the bridge.

Tegan suddenly felt elated.

She felt strong, powerful.

Ready for any sort of action.

But where was this coming from?

This wasn't her at all.

She wondered whether, without knowing, she had absorbed something toxic in the warehouse when she was struck by the Dalek. She had travelled down the time corridor, most of the journey semi-conscious. Had something happened then? Or was it the time when the rogue policemen had walked her back to the warehouse. Even worse, had she been duplicated?

Tegan glanced over her shoulder at the two policemen. There was no denying they were real enough.

As the barge moved closer, Tegan leapt onto the handrail and arm-over-arm lowered herself under one of the bascule leaves.

As the barge chugged out under the bridge on its way to the Thames Barrier and estuary, Tegan released her grasp and managed to drop onto the canvas cover of the vessel.

There she sat, cross-legged like a petite elf.

Totally amazed at what she had just done, Tegan felt empowered, invigorated. She couldn't wait to find out what else she could do. Perhaps she would go after the Dalek duplicates herself? Maybe she had a chance now to make a difference on her own terms …

The two policemen, their expressions implacable, watched from the bridge as the barge continued on its way. They had never seen anything quite like that before.

Since their last encounter with Tegan, she appeared to have acquired skills verging on superpowers. It was therefore imperative she was captured so they could discover just how this had happened.

But first it was time to tell Mr Lytton …

Coming soon from BBC Books

The Target Storybook

by Simon Guerrier, Terrance Dicks, Matthew Sweet, Susie Day, Matthew Waterhouse, Colin Baker, Mike Tucker, Steve Cole, George Mann, Una McCormack, Jenny T. Colgan, Jacqueline Rayner, Beverly Sanford, Vinay Patel and Joy Wilkinson

ISBN 978 1 78594 474 1
£16.99

We're all stories in the end...

In this exciting collection of all-new stories, you'll find unique spin-off tales from some of your favourite *Doctor Who* episodes across the history of the series, such as *War Games, The Lodger* and *Demons of the Punjab*. Prequels, sequels, letters and first-hand accounts from favourite characters, including selections from the Doctor's 500-Year-Diary (and 1,200-Year Diary, and 2,000-Year Diary).

Each story in *The Target Storybook* expands in thrilling ways upon a popular *Doctor Who* adventure. With contributions from show luminaries past and present, *The Target Storybook* is a once-in-a-lifetime tour round the wonders of the Whoniverse.

Gatecrashers
Joy Wilkinson

Journey Out of Terror
Simon Guerrier

Save Yourself
Terrance Dicks

The Clean Air Act
Matthew Sweet

Punting
Susie Day

Dark River
Matthew Waterhouse

Interstitial Insecurity
Colin Baker

The Slyther of Shoreditch
Mike Tucker

We Can't Stop What's Coming
Steve Cole

Decoy
George Mann

Grounded
Una McCormack

The Turning of the Tides
Jenny T. Colgan

Citation Needed
Jacqueline Rayner

Pain Management
Beverly Sanford

Letters from the Front
Vinay Patel

Coming soon from BBC Books

BBC

DOCTOR WHO

Star Tales

by Jenny T. Colgan, Paul Magrs, Jo Cotterill,
Steve Cole, Trevor Baxendale and Mike Tucker

ISBN 978 1 78594 471 0
£12.99

What's in a name?

The Doctor is many things – curious, funny, brave, protective of her friends... and a shameless namedropper. While she and her companions battled aliens and travelled across the universe, the Doctor hinted at a host of previous, untold adventures with the great and the good: we discovered she got her sunglasses from Pythagorus (or was it Audrey Hepburn?); lent a mobile phone to Elvis; had an encounter with Ameila Earhart where she discovered that a pencil-thin spider web can stop a plane; had a 'wet weekend' with Harry Houdini, learning how to escape from chains underwater; and more.

In this collection of new stories, *Star Tales* takes you on a rip-roaring ride through history, from 500BC to the swinging 60s, going deeper into the Doctor's notorious name-dropping and revealing the truth behind these anecdotes.

Chasing the Dawn
Jenny T. Colgan

That's All Right, Mama
Paul Magrs

Einstein and the Doctor
Jo Cotterill

Who-Dini
Steve Cole

The Pythagoras Problem
Trevor Baxendale

Mission of the Kaadok
Mike Tucker